There is a thin veil
between life and death

NICOLE PETERSON

ISBN 978-1-955156-92-9 (paperback)
ISBN 978-1-955156-93-6 (hardcover)
ISBN 978-1-956010-48-0 (digital)

Rushmore Press LLC
1 800 460 9188
www.rushmorepress.com

Printed in the United States of America

CHAPTER ONE

Who carries a baby for nine months and then just leaves it? Oh right, the woman who gave birth to me. I was only a few days old in the hospital when social services came to get me. Obviously, I had no idea what was ahead for a baby in a pink cap and wrapped in a hospital blanket.

Do you know what couples want to adopt? They want to adopt newborn babies. So, why then was I never adopted? I asked myself that question a lot as I grew up in the dysfunctional system of the government. It was because I was a defect. At least that was how I felt my entire life. But the truth was that I was born with a rare heart defect. So, it wasn't enough that my bio mom gave me life and then just left me but she also had to give me a fatal heart condition.

The condition is called aortic stenosis. I looked it up later on when I was older. Basically, I didn't have enough valves in my heart to pump blood to the rest of my body. Some children die immediately and some of them live pretty normal lives. I on the other hand was experiencing every symptom there was, which is not ideal when you go from foster home to foster home and have no real home or parents. The first time I would faint or get sent home from school because I had fainted in the lunch line, the foster parents would call social services to find me another home. I was more trouble than I was worth. I should have died but instead, I lived fifteen painful years with this condition. I know I should be grateful for that, but I wasn't. Sometimes, I would lay in a bed or on the floor of a foster home and wish that I had never been born; unfortunately for me, I had been.

Not one couple wanted to adopt me, which was upsetting enough, but being a sick, parentless child made me feel even worse. So yes, I guess everyone thought that I was way more trouble than I was worth. I'm shocked someone never ended up killing me. The physical abuse in some of these homes was ridiculous. Not only the foster parents but also the older children were always bullying the younger ones.

When I was only about five, there was a boy in one of the homes who always picked on me. I tried to stay out of his way but I remember one day, he wanted to take what I was playing with. It was my favorite toy. It was a red top, one that you spun. This one would light up every time you spun it. It was beautiful and one of the only things that had really made me happy. This boy tried taking it from me and when I went to grab it back from him, he stood up over me and kicked me in the face, shoes and all.

After that, my cheek was bruised under my right eye and the foster parents never said anything. To me, it was a very intense memory that I can never let go of. However, the older I got, the more I realized that all these people wanted was more money from the state. No one really cared about me. I learned that from a young age, so that became my reality. No one cared about me, so I was determined never to care about anyone else.

However, there was one person who always seemed to be there for me and in a miraculous way, he helped me with all of my pain, emotional and physical. So, ever since I could remember, I had one person who loved me.

His name was Ian and even as a child, I was developing a theory that he was my very own guardian angel if you believe in that sort of thing. I'm not sure where I came up with that theory at such a young age, perhaps it was just wishful thinking on my part. But there was something different about Ian. In a room full of children, no one could ever see or hear him except for me. It seemed as though he was invisible to them. I know this because there were many times when the older kids would come up to me and tell me to keep it down while Ian was sitting right there next to me. The first time that happened, I was shocked and then I just got used to it. That was when I began to develop my theory about Ian.

How could I really complain? When I would wake up in so much pain that I couldn't breathe let alone cry for help, Ian was suddenly there sitting by my side with his kind eyes and his cheerful smile, the kind of smile that was so contagious I couldn't help but smile back. Even that tiny smile helped the excruciating pain start to lift. I went suffering from being unable to breathe to feeling very sharp pain.

He would touch my shoulders and start breathing slowly. Soon, the rhythm of my breathing would combine with his and everything would slow down. My lungs would open up and all of the pain would start to fade. My chest would stop hurting and he would just say over and over, "Breathe, baby girl, just breathe." Even the sound of his voice calmed me down. When I wanted to keep crying, I would force myself to breathe with him. I think in some small way, I wanted to make him happy. After all, he made me happy all of the time.

When I was sad, he was there to cheer me up and wipe my tears. He was there when I was hurt physically or mentally to tell me that eventually, everything was going to be okay. Looking back, I'm not sure why I believed him; I just did. Maybe it was the innocence of a child, an innocence that I would definitely grow out of.

I remember one night, I couldn't breathe. I started to cry out but I couldn't. Ian was right there. He sat on my bed with me and gathered me into his arms. There were five other children in that bedroom and no one ever noticed me let alone him. As soon as I was in his arms, my chest opened up again. I laid against his chest with his strong arms holding me tight. "Breathe, baby girl. Can you breathe for me?" I nodded and I felt so much better.

"Ian," I said looking up at him little and wide-eyed.

"Yes, Lily?" I could even hear the smile in his voice.

"Can we play a game?" I asked. I think at that time, I was trying to distract myself.

"Of course, we can, baby girl. What would you like to play?" His voice was sweet like honey. He was genuine in every word he spoke.

"Truth or dare," I said. I had heard about the game from one of the older kids.

"Truth or dare?" He asked sounding amused. I could hear the smile in his voice even though I wasn't looking at him. I was curled up against his chest where I usually was.

"Yes," I said sounding determined.

I was only five then and I had no idea what I was really talking about but I wanted to know more about Ian. Ian always told me the truth. I remember always being happy when I was with him. I remember that he was a handsome man with dark hair and piercing green eyes that were unforgettable. At least I thought they were. He was a grown-up but I thought nothing of his age. It was as if his presence with me was completely normal.

"Yes," he answered almost with a chuckle and then said, "The dare part would be a little difficult." I was too young to even understand what he meant by that. But my curious little brain pressed into asking the questions that I wanted to know.

"Are you an angel?" I asked.

"Yes, I am," he answered so matter of factly that even at five years old, I was startled to hear the answer. But, Ian always told me the truth. He was the one ever who did, I think. Everyone else told me how much they cared about me, but the older I got, the more I realized that was a lie.

"Truth?" I asked.

"Yes, truth." He nodded his head with a very kind and sincere look on his face.

"My turn," he said. He paused and tapped his forefinger on his chin like he was really thinking of a good one. "What do you want to be when you grow up?" His tone was so serious. He sounded genuinely curious.

"I want to be an angel just like you," I smiled proudly. He smiled back and tousled my mess of long blonde hair.

"What's your favorite color?" I asked next.

"Blue," he answered, "like the sky on a clear day." We didn't have too many clear days in Seattle.

I had to think about it for a minute. There were so many colors that I loved. I finally answered with, "Red. My turn." I answered bouncing up and down the bed excited. I was curious about everything and my brain was a little sponge.

"Why can I see you?" I asked.

"Because I am here to help you," he answered.

"Help me with what?" I asked. He did not answer; instead, he just smiled. Yet, there was something about the way he looked at me. He really seemed to care about what happened to me.

We often sat outside in the park by the market. One day, I was chattering about my life and how I wish that I had never been born.

"Why can't I just find parents who love me?" I asked looking up at him with tears in my eyes. He looked at me so sadly that day. I had never seen him sad before.

"Lily," he started, "you are a very special girl and there is a plan for your life." He sounded so sure.

"How do you know?" I swung my feet back and forth under the bench.

"Because I'm your angel. I'm supposed to know these things; now, shall we?" He stood up and put his hand out for me to take. I took it and jumped off of our bench. I wondered what it looked like to people when I took Ian's hand since technically, he wasn't there.

We walked through the outdoor market with its vendors set up everywhere selling jewelry, paintings, flowers, and such. It was such a huge tourist attraction that I almost always nearly got knocked over onto the ground. We walked past all the vendors outdoor to walk into more vendors under a huge tent. I always loved the market though, but my favorite part was all the fresh seafood that would come in right from the docks. Sometimes, I would watch them taking the lobsters and the crabs off the boat. I often wondered how they could catch so many.

We would walk past all of the people and I would look at the handmade dreamcatchers and homemade jewelry. Sometimes, I would stop and look at the rings that people had made out of shells or some kind of natural stone. It was so tight in there but I would get moved along by the crowd.

There were big crabs spread out over ice. I would look at all of the fresh fish and lobsters. I always saw the sign for oysters and wondered what they tasted like. I thought that one day, I would buy some.

I went through many different foster homes in Seattle, Washington as if I was not depressed enough about my life. *Here*, the entire city was depressed. There were people in local parks being pulled out daily for overdosing on something.

We were lucky if we saw the sun on a good day in March. Plus, it's just gross and damp all of the time. There are so many people depressed here. I was one of them. Sometimes, I wondered why the kids in the park did what they did. Did it help?

It didn't matter then because I had Ian and he was the little hope that I had. One day when I was about seven, Ian and I sat down on a bench in our park. Half of the park was for kids to swing and play on the monkey bars. The other half was a big pond with benches. It was quiet and peaceful to me, even though really, there were so many people around.

"Lily," he started. This could not be good but at the time, I didn't know what to expect. "Soon, you will forget me. Your innocence will run out and you won't see me or even remember me anymore." He had looked so sad and at seven years old, I was very confused. Tears came to my eyes.

"Why?" It was the mind of a child and the older I got, the less I would think like a child. I know that now, but of course, I didn't then. My eyes were wide and I was scared of being without him.

"But I'm not afraid when you are here." I was young but smart.

"You will be okay, baby girl, and I will always be with you," he said

"But how will you always be with me if you are going away?" I looked up at him with tears in my eyes.

How? How was it going to be ok? He was the only one who helped me when my heart started to shut down. I didn't think anyone else would have cared if I died. It would be less trouble, right? One less mouth to feed. One less child in the system. But Ian cared and helped me, so what would happen to me?

"It is hard to explain to you now, sweet girl." He lightly touched the top of my head. "I am not leaving now. I will just fade in time from your memory." He took my small hand in his.

"If you leave, who will help me?" I was urgent and scared. Just then, the sun peaked out from behind a cloud over the sound and I could feel its warmth on my cheek. I lived for those moments when the sun would come out. But I was always there in the park by the market, sitting on that old wooden bench with my best friend, my only friend, so right then, I could not imagine being without him.

"I will always be here to help you. Please don't be afraid, Lily. You are strong, always remember that." I remember that he just continued to be with me until he wasn't. After that, I did not remember that he ever existed. I did feel alone! But that was my life. I had no friends because I was moving around so much that I stopped caring to even make any family love me. There is some self-pity for you but I didn't care because there was no one to care about, until the day I met *him.*

CHAPTER TWO

I was fifteen and living in a crappy house with crappy people who just wanted money. One day, my social worker showed up at the house. That was unexpected; she never just showed up like that. I was sitting on the steps of the front porch. There were toys all over the front lawn and it was a small house. I shared a small room with two other girls who were younger than me. I had no room to breathe in there! So, I spent a lot of time outside.

"Hello, Lily," she stopped, probably waiting for a response that never came. I just looked at her and so she went on, "Lily, I have a home for you. There is a spot that opened up and the family wanted to help another child." Help . . . I almost laughed in her face. "I know how cramped you are here." She motioned. My social worker was a beautiful African-American woman, her hair and makeup were always beautiful, and she always wore really nice pantsuits that showed off her slender body. She had been my social worker since I was five. I wanted to be nice to her but I wasn't so nice to anyone anymore.

"When?" I asked.

"Today." She smiled at me and I tried to smile back. "Go get your things." She seemed pleased, which made me wonder where she was taking me. I grabbed a pillowcase and threw in some t-shirts and some underwear and that was it. I was too used to moving. It was sad really, but as I said, this was my life. I was already wearing my favorite pair of jeans. I left the room without looking back.

Dina was talking to the foster mother when I came back down. Dina. That was her name. I never used it though. We said a short goodbye and I left yet another place behind. She drove to a really nice part of the city. The lawns were green and groomed. It was springtime so I could see some of the flowers coming to life. However, I was surprised by where we were going. If my new home was here, they certainly did not need the money.

The house was beautiful. It was painted white with light blue shudders. There was a two-car garage and the front lawn was almost covered with shrubs and flowers. There was even a big wooden front porch with a porch swing. Disgustingly perfect. That was my thought too.

The social worker rang the bell and a minute later, a slender blonde-haired lady answered the door. She was plain but a little pretty. She had no make-up on and she only wore jeans and a white t-shirt. She smiled at both of us. Her fingernails had dirt under them like she had been working in the garden.

"Hi, Dina." She said still smiling. Of course, they knew each other. I rolled my eyes. I was never in the mood to meet new people. What was the point? They would get rid of me anyway as soon as they realized how much trouble I would be.

It isn't that I didn't want a home; it was my disease that people couldn't stand. I was always falling downstairs, ending up in the nurse's office at school, or being sent home for passing out. Since the state didn't send extra money for their troubles, my social worker was always finding me new homes. I used to feel bad for her when I was younger. Eventually, I stopped feeling bad for anyone. Life sucks and people just had to deal with it, or I did anyway.

"Dawn, it is so good to see you again." Dina smiled back.

The woman turned to me and smiled, "You must be Lily."

"That's me," I replied more than a little uncomfortable. She opened the door inviting us in. The house was complete with hardwood floors as we walked into a small foyer. As we walked down the hallway, I glanced for a second at the small sitting room full of antique furniture. I was positive that nobody actually *sat* in there. At the end of the narrow hallway, the room opened up into a large living room and kitchen area. There was a sliding glass door that led out to more gardens and flowers.

"Please sit down." She motioned to a large plush sofa that I swear I could have lived on. I looked around and saw toys for a small girl and to my right, the room was complete with a fireplace. There had to be something wrong here because this was too good to be true. We sat there far longer than I wanted to while my new foster mother and the social worker sat there chatting.

I felt relieved when I sensed the needless chatter coming to an end. Finally! I thought to myself. But what was I really that eager to do? I think I had just wanted to be alone. I should have known better than that. I was in a foster home. I was never alone, but this time, I would welcome the company I was about to meet.

Dina stood up. "Well, that is all then. Lily is a great girl." She said, putting her arm on my shoulder. I cringed at the physical contact at first and then let my dear social worker give me a little squeeze as if she would never see me again. I had to admit that she had never done that before. She waved goodbye and I waved back.

There I stood alone with this woman. She smiled at me from across the room on the other sofa. She must have read my face because she suddenly got up. "Would you like to see your room?"

She kept smiling and I know she was trying to make me comfortable but it only made me more uncomfortable.

The foster mother started up the steep staircase that was right off the living area and so I followed behind. I never used people's names. What's the point? You learn a name and then you leave anyway.

The room that I was going to be staying in was at the end of the hall. Right as we got into the doorway, she put her hands on her hips. "Jason, get out of here." She sounded annoyed but it was an annoyance that I could tell she was used to. At least, that's how it sounded to me. I was stupid to think that I would actually get a minute alone in a foster home.

From the doorway, I could see a full-sized bed covered in a dark purple comforter with lilac pillowcases. On the other side of the room, I saw a bed that looked exactly the same, only smaller. There were purple rugs beside each bed on the hardwood floor. This was the nicest home I had ever been in. I assumed that the bed the boy was sitting on was supposed to be for me. There he was! He was cute. That was all I could think. He was cute with radiant blue eyes and short blonde hair. He looked about my age or maybe a little older.

He just stared at her like he had not heard a word she just said. After a minute or so, she threw up her hands and turned to walk away.

"I trust you two will get acquainted." She called over her shoulder. I was pretty sure it was more for his benefit than for mine. I stood there for a second taking him in. Yes, he was cute but there was something more that I couldn't put my finger on. There was something that seemed so familiar to me. It was like I already knew him.

I gathered myself together and walked over to the bed, pillowcase in hand. I sat down next to him still holding my pillowcase. The pillowcase was sacred. I had been using it since I was little. I couldn't remember when or what house I had taken it from. I just didn't remember ever being without it.

We sat there in silence not looking at one another for a while. I did not know what it was about this boy but he completely disarmed me. I sat there feeling angry and sad. I suddenly felt a strange calm come over me. All my anger and bitterness melted away. My whole body was tingling with awareness.

"You travel light." He finally spoke and looked at me. His eyes were smiling but his tone was sarcastic. He reminded me of myself.

"Well, when you travel as much as I do . . ." I trailed off and looked back down at the floor.

"So, you are Lily, huh?" He looked thoughtful and yet mischievous. It was that very quality that he possessed that I loved about him. It was like he was sincere but always kept you guessing. I liked that about him. I liked everything about him so far, but I couldn't let my guard down. Not with anyone, I had to remind myself.

"That's me," I answered sarcastically.

"What a beautiful name for such a miserable girl," he smirked. Was he just trying to get a rise out of me? Because apparently, it had worked.

"I am not miserable!" I started to get defensive and there it was, that mischievous smile that completely disarmed me. Great, I thought, rolling my eyes. Not only could he render me speechless but he could also get to me. I couldn't help but smile back. "Fine," I conceded, "I am miserable, but can you blame? Jason, right?"

"That's me," he mocked my tone. I glared at him but it was so hard to be mad at that face. I was almost mad at myself for liking a boy. It sounded ridiculous but I had never really noticed a boy before. Now I was sitting here being forced to.

"Why are you sitting on *my* bed?" I demanded all of a sudden feeling very uncomfortable. I never felt comfortable with anyone. It was almost like he could feel my uncertainty. He stood up turning to face me.

"Why not?" He gave me a crooked smile. He turned around and left without another word. I almost wanted him to come back. What was happening to me? Was this normal? Was this how other girls felt when they had a crush on a boy? I rolled my eyes at myself. Did I have a crush on a boy I just laid eyes on? In the middle of me beating myself up, he popped his head back in.

"Do you even like purple?" He smiled and pointed around the room.

"Red," I answered, "crimson maybe." I smiled back and for the first time in my life, I felt like I had a friend. I sighed throwing myself back onto the bed. I felt happy and it felt good. I let myself smile for once.

After an hour, I heard voices coming up the stairs. It was the foster mother with the cutest little red-headed girl.

"Let me introduce you to her." She was talking to the little girl.

"Lily, this is Ruby. You two will be sharing this room." Ruby was wearing a long shirt with black tights under it. She was so little and yet looked so grown up. Her beautiful red hair was pulled back in a ponytail and her cheeks were round and freckles.

"Hi, Ruby," I smiled and she did a half-smile back.

"Hi," she said shyly. I wondered who had lived here before.

"Well, Lily, that is about it. You and Ruby are in here and Jason is in the room next door. Let me know if he gives you any trouble." She said and stared at me thoughtfully for a moment before turning around to go back downstairs. That was weird. Ruby did not go with her. I would have thought that she would want to play with all of those toys downstairs. There was one thing that I learned quickly—Ruby was actually a really good friend.

I sat on the edge of my bed and watched as she sat on her own bed facing me. I wasn't sure what to say but I had to at least be friendly with her. No matter the age difference, we still shared a room. I did not want to be mean to her like so many kids had been to me.

"How old are you?" It came out nice but it could have been softer, except I was not a soft person.

"I am six," she answered and she sat up a little straighter. Then she surprised me.

"How old are you?" she asked me sounding so grown up.

"I am fifteen." I watched her put her head down.

"Do you like living here, Ruby?" I asked as gently as I could. Something in this house seemed too perfect to me.

"I love my mom and dad," she answered. The statement made me catch my breath. I had assumed that she was a foster child like me.

"Oh," was all I could say for a minute. "So, you're not a foster child?" I asked still stunned.

"Nope," she said with a little grin. It was an innocent grin. I had seen six-year-olds grin in much worse ways. Ruby seemed happy and it made me smile a little.

We were called to dinner and I met Mark, the foster father. He was for the most part very handsome. I suspected that he looked younger than he was. He was fair-skinned and I saw where Ruby got her red hair from.

"You must be Lily." He stared at me. Why did everyone keep saying that? Couldn't people just introduce themselves? I was getting annoyed and I think he could tell because the next words that came out of his mouth were, "Have a seat. Dawn is a great cook." He smiled again but this time, I couldn't help but not like the way he looked at me. I couldn't put my finger on it. I just felt a tug in my stomach.

We all sat down at the very nice dining table and ate together. Mark never looked at Jason during dinner. I remember thinking that it was strange. He didn't really even acknowledge his presence. It didn't seem to bother Jason though, although nothing seemed to bother Jason.

"She is only doing this for you," Jason who was sitting next to me, leaned in and whispered.

"No whispering, Jason, and I heard you." She winked at me. "I wanted a special night for you, Lily." Jason threw her a look that could kill. Nope, I was not imagining it. Something was off. I was happy to be sitting next to Jason. He felt safe to me. We had just met and I did not want to leave his side. Most people would say that I had a teenage crush and that it was completely normal. But I did not have crushes and this boy was definitely not normal.

"I am in no need of any special attention," I said. I thought I saw a small smile from the foster father out of the corner of my eye. Jason stiffened and *that* I was not making up. It was very clear to me that something was going on between them.

Ruby was so quiet at the table. Was she always this quiet? She did talk some in our room. After dinner, I let her change into her pajamas alone. I was standing outside of the room with my arms folded when the door to Jason's room opened and he peaked his head out. I almost could not help smiling but I was able to restrain myself.

"What are you doing?" I asked in a whisper.

"Looking at you." And there it was, he disarmed me and I smiled. Now I *was* a silly girl. I furrowed my eyebrows and glared at him.

"Ok, bitter girl." He winked at me and went back into his room. What was that? I met this boy today and he was paying so much attention to me. And I liked it! I do not like people and I do not get to know people. To my experience, it is never worth it.

Ruby opened the door in cute little fairy pajamas. I came into the room and laid down on my bed in my jeans and t-shirt. I didn't own any pajamas, so I laid there thinking about *Jason*. He was in the next room, so close to me. I felt my entire body tingle.

I looked over at Ruby who was turning on her night light and getting into bed. I smiled at her. She was so sweet and innocent-looking until she spoke.

"Are you happy to be here?" Ruby asked me from her bed.

"I think so. I only just got here." I paused for a moment. "What about you? Are you happy that I'm here?" I was curious about this little girl who looked so innocent and yet has something behind her eyes.

"You seem nice." She sounded sad. "But sometimes, I have nightmares, so I don't like the night."

"I get nightmares too, Ruby." I wanted to reassure her. Her statement sounded so dark and afraid, just another weird and creepy thing to add to my list of weird things about this house. The only one who seemed a little normal was Jason.

"Goodnight, Lily," she said to me and rolled over. I looked at her little shape in the glow of her night light. She had a story. Every one of us had a story and I could not help but wonder what hers was. I supposed I would find that out in time. I sighed, turning over and closing my eyes. My first night in a new place, again.

CHAPTER THREE

"Lily!" I felt someone shaking me and heard my name. It took me a minute to realize where I was. I opened my eyes and all I saw was Jason and the glow of Ruby under her night light. I must have fallen asleep.

"Get up, come on." He looked at me and then offered me his hand. For a second, I grabbed at my chest. He must have noticed because he paused for a second.

"Are you ok?" He asked looking concerned.

"I think so. What time is it?" I took his hand and the pain slowed to a stop. He still hadn't answered my question, which I learned was typical of Jason. It was frustrating and also endearing to me at the same time.

"Where are we going?" I whispered as loud as I could. He didn't answer me. We just kept going. We snuck out the back door and I saw him go between the trash cans and pull out a glass bottle.

"What is that?" He put a finger to his lips to silence me. Then took my hand again and pulled me along.

"Where are we going?" I demanded.

"Somewhere that you can relax!" He sounded urgent and somehow annoyed at the same time.

"Why do you think I need to relax?" I snapped. "You have known me for what? Like five seconds?"

"Oh, shut up!" he snapped back. "You have had a hard life . . . blah, blah, blah!" He rolled his eyes at me. I was so taken back that I had nothing to say. Who did he think he was? He didn't even know me! I wanted to be angry but I wasn't. He was right. It was just that no one had ever called me on it before. Here I was, following a boy I really didn't know and never felt so understood before in my life. That was the thing about Jason. He could always render me speechless. I hated that!

We snuck around the house and once we were far enough away, we both straightened up and kept walking. I was still wondering where we were going but I did not ask again. He let go of my hand then and I kept walking right beside him. It was hard to keep up though and I was starting to feel dizzy.

"I can hear you thinking from here." He smirked.

"I am just wondering where we are going, that's all." I raised an eyebrow.

"Right here." He pointed to the park. It was literally a park with slides, monkey bars, and swings. I loved swings! They always calmed me down. I always felt free as the wind would hit my face and the up and down motion was just calming. I smiled and walked faster toward them.

"So, you like the swings?" He sat down on one and shook the one beside him for me to sit down.

"I love to swing!" I smiled. Then my eyes focused on the bottle in his hand. "So, what are we doing?" I was cautious. He started laughing.

"This, baby girl, is our relaxation." He held up the bottle and I was bothered by him calling me baby girl. It was too familiar, but I couldn't figure out why. Maybe it was all just a dream from a long time ago. He offered me the bottle and I hesitated.

"Haven't you ever drank before?" He looked so shocked I almost laughed at him.

"No." I looked at the bottle. I had heard a lot about drinking alcohol, but never had the guts to try it. Perhaps, it had something to do with my heart condition. I was curious though so I took it from him. I hesitated before taking a small swig.

"Oh, just drink it!" He nudged me.

"You are a bad influence!" I pushed him back smiling. I couldn't help it. I had smiled more today than I had in my entire life. I would be sad to leave here.

"I'm good at that." He sounded light and almost proud of himself. I took another drink and then spit a little out. It was awful! He started laughing. He must have seen the look on my face.

"This is awful!" I exclaimed. I looked over at him with a sour look on my face. "Why are you laughing at me?" I practically whined in his direction. I wanted to laugh too but I couldn't help watching how graceful he looked as he put the bottle to his lips and took a swig like it was nothing.

"And how exactly is this supposed to relax me?" I asked, squinting my eyes at him. I was still skeptical of him in some way. Why shouldn't I be? I didn't really know him yet.

"Here," he handed the bottle back to me. "Take another sip and you'll see." He was right. That next swig went down smoother, but it was the after-effect that was unforgettable to me. I felt all warm inside and just a little more relaxed. I took another sip. This time, I could barely taste it anymore and I relaxed into the swing feeling calm.

"Give it back!" He grabbed the bottle back and I giggled a little.

"And there it is." He looked at me. "Ladies and gentleman, I got the angry girl to relax." He raised his hands up to an invisible crowd.

"I am *not* angry," I smirked. I could not control myself, but I didn't care. He was right, I needed to relax. I had needed to relax my whole life. This must have been why all of those kids in the park did what they did. The feeling was amazing. For the first time ever, I was not thinking about how much I hated everyone and everything. I was having fun!

"Ok," I said, "now I understand." I had never felt peace like this before. I had never felt peace at all. I was angry at everyone and everything. I could not wait to turn eighteen and get a place of my own.

He handed me the bottle again. This time, it went down smoothly and I closed my eyes taking it all in.

"I still cannot believe that you have never had a drink before." He teased, giving me a cute crooked smile that I hadn't noticed before. He playfully took the bottle from me.

"Really?" I said sarcastically. "When would I get an opportunity to drink?"

"You are a foster kid. I am willing to bet that you would have been able to get out plenty of times!" He challenged me.

"Well, I didn't," I paused, holding his gaze for just a second, "drink, I mean. Of course, I was able to get out on my own. No one cared where I was." I felt a little dizzy but in a good way. I stared at him for a moment. He looked so comfortable on the swing. I had never felt anything for a boy before, probably because I just stayed away from anybody at all costs. I am positive that wasn't healthy but it was how I coped.

"So, what is your story then?" he asked.

"My story?" I tried to concentrate and this was all I could get out. "My birth mother left when I was born. I have not one but two heart defects which are most likely why no one ever wanted to adopt me and I have been living like this my whole life. Oh, I forgot, I probably should be dead." I looked at him sideways and smiled.

"So, what's your deal?" I asked smirking at him.

"I don't really have one," For a second, he looked sad. "My parents died a long time ago and I don't have any family. So . . ." he trailed off.

"You don't have any other family?" I pushed. I never really talked to anyone so it wasn't like I had many social skills. However, the alcohol seemed to be helping with that.

"No," he shrugged. He closed down, leaving me even more curious but not wanting to upset him, so I changed the subject.

"How old are you?" I asked.

"I am seventeen and I will be eighteen in a couple of months." He held his head high. I giggled at him a little. He seemed so proud of himself, like a five-year-old saying how old he was.

"Then what?" I asked.

"Then," he hesitated, "I don't know. Get out of here, that's for sure." He sounded unsure. Was he really unsure of himself? Jason did not strike me as a person who was ever unsure about anything.

"What is your plan?" he asked.

"I want to find my own place," I shrugged. "I, however, do not have the luxury of turning eighteen any time soon." He stared at me for a long moment and I was beginning to wonder what was going on inside of that beautiful mind of his.

"Lily, I kind of like you." He said and that brought a smile to my face.

"You don't even know me," I said looking down. It was dark so maybe he couldn't see me starting to blush. There were butterflies in my stomach! That was something I had never experienced before but just heard from other girls talking about how boys made them feel like they had butterflies in their stomachs. I used to roll my eyes and think that it was all so stupid and yet now, I was experiencing it and it didn't seem stupid at all. It was fun and exciting. I smiled.

"I know enough. I know I see a lot of me in you." He handed me the bottle back. "For only knowing you for five seconds." He mocked me. Jason was always mocking me. I figured out eventually it was because he thought I was funny or dramatic, one of the two.

"Ok, smartypants," I smirked. "I kind of like you too." I looked down at my feet.

"Good." He held up the bottle as if to say cheers.

"So, why don't you have a girlfriend?" I had no idea why those words just fell out of my mouth and wished I could take them back immediately. I never sounded so stupid, or was it that I just never cared before?

"Who says that I don't have a girlfriend?" He was cute when he got defensive.

"Well, do you?" I asked, flirting a little and pulling on his swing.

"No, I don't." He leaned in, putting his forehead close to mine.

"Why not?" I leaned toward him and he was so cute. I wished I could kiss him. What was wrong with me? Does alcohol make you that brave? It must because I almost did kiss him.

"Ok, drinky," he said taking the bottle from me.

"Hey!" I tried to grab the bottle back but he was too fast.

"Get up. It's probably safe to go back now," he said standing over me. I tried to stand and I couldn't. I couldn't stand let alone walk.

"What do you mean it is 'safe' to go back?" I held onto him laughing. I could see that he was laughing too.

"You ask too many questions." That was all the reply that I got that night. That was the night I fell in love, not with Jason but with alcohol. For the first time, I didn't have to feel what I had been feeling my entire life. It was like a huge weight had been lifted from me and it was as simple as taking a sip out of a bottle.

"I could get used to this," I said and then I fell right on my face. Everything went black for a moment. This time, I heard a voice. Had I heard a voice? It was a girl's voice and she sounded urgent.

"I know it's time. I need more time." I could hear her as if she was standing right next to me but I couldn't see her. Who was she talking to? The next thing I knew, I was opening my eyes to Jason standing over me. I decided that I was drunk and hearing things. I let him lift me off of the ground.

"Are you ok?" He looked so worried.

"I am never ok," I replied still drunk. He sighed picking me up and throwing me over his shoulder. I made a little squeak but no attempt to struggle. He took me all the way to my bed and put me under my covers. "I don't like this color," I half whined.

"I know, sweet girl." He stroked my hair softly. "Red. No, crimson." I remember him kissing my forehead. Was he like this with all of the other girls who lived here before me?

CHAPTER FOUR

The next morning, I felt someone shaking me again. This time, it was the foster mother. I opened my eyes and glared. I was not a morning person at all.

"Lily, honey, you have your first day of school today." She looked happy.

Great, I thought to myself. Another school to go to and ignore everybody. I hated school. I put my face in my pillow and moaned. My head was pounding! I waited for her to leave the room before sitting up. I looked not seeing Ruby anywhere. She must already have gotten up. I walked to the bathroom still in the clothes from the night before. Really, they were the only clothes I owned. I did look into the pillowcase and found one clean dark blue t-shirt. Just as I was closing the door to the bathroom, a hand stopped it. I jumped a little startled but there he was standing in the doorway.

"Do you have any boundaries?" My eyes were still half closed and I sounded crabby. That was normal, though. I was always crabby in the morning. I just did not usually have to deal with anyone.

"No," Jason answered straight-faced. I loved when he did that. I had to stop myself from laughing. He could say the ridiculous thing with the straightest face—just one of the many qualities that I was learning to love about him at the time.

"Drink this and take these." He handed me a cup of coffee and two pills that I assumed were for my pounding headache. "I will be downstairs," he said and then just walked away. I closed the door and took a sip of the coffee. It was good. Why was he so attached to me already? It didn't matter because the thought of him caring gave me butterflies. Nice, Lily, so much for not getting attached to anyone, especially him! He would be gone in a couple of months anyway, and I would be left alone again. I closed my eyes trying to shake off the sadness that I felt when I now thought of him leaving and got into the shower. I didn't have anything! I didn't have clothes or a book bag. I went downstairs and saw Jason sitting on the sofa. I smiled at him as I walked over to the counter to put my coffee cup down.

"Ready to go?" Jason asked me standing up. I looked at him confused. What did he mean? Just as I was about to say something to him, the foster mother walked into the room. "Ready to go where?" she asked. She must have heard him from the other room.

"I am taking her to school." Again, she just stared at him like she wanted to say something but couldn't. It was weird and so it caught my attention. It was as if she took orders from him. Why was she afraid to challenge him? Yet, she still raised her eyebrows at him.

"I swear! I am taking her to school." He put up both of his hands in surrender. "This is all new to her and I'm sure the last thing she wants to do is take the bus alone. Right, Lily?" His eyes widened at me to agree with him.

"Yes, of course. I don't want to take a bus." I faked a small smile at her.

"I see the two of you did get acquainted then. Ok, then." She looked skeptical but did not argue about it any further. Again, she did not argue with him, and yet, she seemed wary of him.

"Are you hungry?" she asked me, still smiling. "I have breakfast." Ugh. The thought of eating made my tummy turn. Jason saw the look in my eyes. He started to grab my hand and then stopped himself.

"No, I am not very hungry this morning." That was all I said in true Lily style.

"Before you go." She walked over to the sofa and picked up an expensive-looking brown book bag. "Here," she said holding it out to me, "I thought maybe you needed one." I actually smiled at her.

"Thank you," I said very surprised. Maybe she wasn't all that bad.

"You are welcome," she smiled back. "Well, you better get going." She was so nice but the last thing I wanted was to get close, so I just turned to Jason instead of saying another word to her and we started out toward the door.

Once we were outside, I got to see his little beater car. It was an awful brown Toyota. I laughed to myself but I did have to give him credit though. He kept a clean car. We drove for a while and then came to a high school. The school wasn't big but it wasn't small either and my heart started to race.

"You are really taking me to school?" I asked, my heart beating faster. I felt my body getting faint.

"Hey," he said soothingly without skipping a beat. "He grabbed my hand. I'm here, ok? Can you breathe for me, Lily?" I felt a calm come over me as soon as he touched me. That was new. I nodded and looked into his eyes. Those eyes had so many stories to tell but most importantly, those eyes always kept me from losing my mind! He was the only one who could ever calm me down. Jason fixed it. That's what he did. He always swooped in and fixed me.

"O-K?" He enunciated each syllable. "I will be here as soon as you come out."

"Fine." I playfully acted annoyed. I looked down and he was still holding my hand. When he didn't make a move to let go, I pulled it back. I got out of the car and did not look back. It was a pleasant-looking campus with benches outside in grassy areas. I was so nervous but I just kept walking until I reached the doors. Looking back, he was still sitting there. I felt the butterflies again and went into the clean school swarming with kids that I had no interest in getting to know.

When school was finally over and I had successfully avoided almost everyone that I came in contact with, I could not help but practically run outside. As promised, Jason was sitting outside in his car right after school. I smiled and tried not to run to the car, but I was so happy to see him. Why? I had barely known him. Yet, there he was, my life preserver.

"How was your first day of school?" He smiled at me. I glared back at him. "That good, huh?" He winked with a smile. I hated him for mocking me.

"It was fine." I sighed. "Just another school."

"I love what a happy person you are," he smirked at me. I shoved his shoulder and we both started laughing. There it was straight face, ridiculous thing.

"Thanks for picking me up though," I said smiling over at him. Something about this boy made me incredibly happy and incredibly stressed out all at the same time and I could not figure out why.

"And ah, thanks, hmmm . . . I must be getting on your good side." I just shook my head. I felt like I could never risk losing Jason. We had a connection that I never had before and until now, I never knew that I needed it.

"Do you want to go back to the house?" He glanced at me as he pulled out of the school parking lot.

I didn't answer him right away. Instead, I held up the book bag, "Is this weird? Or does she do this for *all* of the other girls?"

"There were no other girls," he said solemnly.

"There were no other foster girls?" I was confused. "Then, why are there two beds in there?"

"They had another daughter. She was about fifteen when she died." He kept driving but he wasn't heading back toward the house.

"How did she die?" I wasn't sure that I wanted to know because I was apparently living in her room.

"She killed herself." He sighed.

"Why did she kill herself?" I asked, completely surprised. Those weren't the words I was expecting to come out of his mouth.

"I don't know." But I could see pain behind his eyes.

"Did you know her?" I asked. I felt bad for all of them instantly, including Jason.

"Yes," he said, then seemed closed off and I wondered what had happened, but I didn't want to push him any more than that right now.

"Subject change?"

"Yes, please." We both laughed. "I'm taking you to coffee downtown."

"Starbucks?" I asked excitedly. I had not had Starbucks since I was a little girl but I remembered I was liking it a lot.

"Lily, you do know that we live in Seattle, right?"

"Yea, yea," I said rolling my eyes at him. If it was that easy to love after knowing someone only a day, then how much more attached was I going to get? That scared me because he would turn eighteen soon and leave me just like everybody else did. I pushed that thought out of my head and had amazing coffee with the cutest boy I knew.

As soon as we got back to the house, I went upstairs to my room. To my surprise, Ruby was there. She was playing with her dolls and did not seem to notice me walk in. I put my books down on the made-up bed that I swear I hadn't made this morning. Ruby looked up at me smiling.

"Hey, Ruby." I sat down on the floor next to her. I lazily picked up one of her dolls. They looked nice and very expensive. She was so cute with her red hair in little ringlets. I may be bitter and angry at the world, but I had always been good with kids. Some of the children I lived with were lucky that I had been there from time to time. I would never let anyone hurt them the way I had been hurt.

For some reason, Ruby was so much more likable than any other kid. She seemed much more grown-up to me than she actually was. I had to watch what I said to her and remember that she was still only six.

"How was your day?" I asked after sitting there for a moment, trying to avoid my homework. I was finally getting a grip on this weird feeling that I had about this house. After what Jason had just told me, I understood a little more, but still, there was this nagging feeling. I got up and squatted down beside her.

"It was good. How was yours?" she asked so sweetly and like a little grown-up. She looked up and smiled. It was such an obvious answer and a really stupid question but I couldn't think of anything to say to her.

"It wasn't so bad." Again, reminding myself that she was only six. She just seemed so much older and wiser than that. "Ruby, is it ok with you that I moved into your room?"

"I didn't mind when Jason moved in," she started. "It is nice having you here." Then she went back to playing with her dolls. She did not really answer my question. But she was so little I didn't want to upset her, so I just softly touched one of her little perfect ringlets and walked back over to my bed.

I walked over to my bed and opened my book bag pulling out my brand-new books. I sat on my bed for about an hour going over physics homework and English, which wasn't so bad. I actually kind of liked both subjects. It was a new school and yet again, I was the new girl. However, the teachers seemed to feel bad for me, so I didn't get as much homework. It was a public school but it was the nicest one that I had ever been to—no metal detectors and everything was clean. There were tons of vending machines around the entire school and all the classrooms looked like they all had new equipment and such. I supposed I could have been stuck in a worse school. *That's right, I already I had been*, I thought rolling my eyes to myself.

The next day was the same drill, hungover from hanging out with Jason the night before, and then he took me to school and picked me up. That day, we actually went home. I had been on my bed staring at a physics paper for about fifteen minutes when his majesty poked his head in our room.

"Hi, Ruby!" Jason said vibrantly smiling. I looked up glad for the distraction.

"Hi, Jason!" she said smiling back. "Do you want to play dolls with me?" she asked him excitedly.

"I can't right now, little one, but save a spot for me at the tea table. Right next to princess Ella." He had the biggest, most genuine smile on his face and the biggest heart. Maybe he and I really were a lot alike.

"Ok, I will," she replied and went back to her dolls.

"What are you doing right now?" he asked

"Me?"

"Yes, *you*!" He made a face at me and I glared back at him.

"I'm doing my homework, why?" I looked into his eyes, then quickly looked away.

"Seriously?" he asks, making a face at me. It was a cute playful one, not that all of his looks weren't cute. "Well, cut it out. Let's go!" He looked so excited I couldn't say no. In fact, I don't think I ever said no to Jason. If there was such a thing as loving someone unconditionally, then he was that person for me. He could do anything to me and I would probably just keep loving him anyway.

"We just got home like an hour ago," I tried protesting, but like I said, there was no arguing with that boy.

We got into his car and drove for a long time. The earth was green and the trees were tall and strong. I could feel safe here, or maybe I just felt safe with Jason here. He finally stopped the car at a small bridge over a lake and got out.

"Are you coming or what?" He gestured with his arms backing slowly away from me.

"I am!" I yelled back, walking quickly to catch up. "I am here." I stood next to him as we looked out onto the lake. Then he turned and went back to the car.

"What are you doing?" I called after him, then I saw it—the bottle of whiskey. Only this time, he brought cups. He sat up on the very unsteady-looking railing on the little bridge and looked at me.

"Wow, you brought cups," was all I could think to say. I watched him pour straight whiskey into both cups.

"Come on," he said, patting the railing beside himself.

"You want me to sit up there?" I cocked my head to the side.

"I promise I will not let you fall," he said and gave me a completely heartwarming smile that no normal person would be able to say no to.

"No," I said folding my arms defiantly.

"Fine, more whiskey for me," he retorted.

"You know me too well." I glared at him. "You *promise* that you will not let me fall?"

"Why would I let my best girl get hurt?" I felt warm all over before I even took a sip of whiskey. I still held onto the railing tightly.

I drank and I felt that peace again. I loved that feeling. Jason scooted closer to me as I nervously took another swallow and of course, there went my heart again. Sometimes, it was like my heart brought us together.

"Just breathe, baby girl." He took my hand. This time, I squeezed back and as promised, he got me gently off of the railing.

"It is you," I said softly, not really knowing what I meant.

"What do you mean?" He looked a little startled at first.

"My heart, I mean." I couldn't look at him. "*You* are making my heart race."

"Why, Lily are you saying that I make your heart race?" He grinned.

"That is exactly what I just said." I shook my head at him. "Then my chest begins to hurt."

"I always calm you down though, don't I?" he said with a serious look. "I don't want to lose you now. I only just found you." Then, it was my turn to be surprised. Was all of this flirting more than a little crush? It certainly had been for me, but I could only speak for myself of course.

"Earth to Lily," he was saying and snapped me out of my thoughts.

I jerked my head up. "Yes," I agreed with him, "then you always calm me down." We sat there holding hands for a while. We sat there until I had drunk half of the bottle and he had to carry me to bed. We did this for weeks. Every night, we would go out and sit and talk and he quickly became my best friend.

Until the one night that we did not go out and I had fallen asleep early. I assumed it was Jason and so I sat up. But it was Mark, my foster father. I started to feel sick. He smelled like alcohol but not the whiskey that Jason and I drank.

"Expecting someone else?" he slurred his words. I looked around for a minute not sure what was happening. He got into bed next to me and started kissing me. I leaned away from him.

"It's ok, darling," he slurred again, "just relax." But I didn't relax. I tried and tried to push him away. It didn't stop him. He held me down and put his hands all over me. He touched me where I had never been touched before and I was dying inside. I wanted to scream for help. I wanted to scream for Jason but I couldn't. All I could do was lay there and try not to cry until it was done and then he just got up and walked out.

I turned over and started to cry, not just a few tears but sobs, so I put my face on my pillow. I couldn't move. When I looked up, there was Ruby standing in front of me next to my bed.

"Ruby," I stifled another sob. Oh my God! Ruby was there and she knew what was happening or at least she had some idea. "Bad dream?" I asked. She nodded her head and so I lifted my comforter and she crawled into bed with me that night.

"Yea, me too," I said still stunned.

I held onto her close to me and we both went to sleep. This poor little girl. I could only imagine what was going on in her head. All I knew is that she knew something was wrong. How often had she witnessed this, or worse, did he do it to her? Now I thought I had an understanding of what was going on between Jason and the foster parents. I thought that now maybe I understood what had happened to their other daughter.

CHAPTER FIVE

The next day after a very long, hot shower I walked into Jason's room for a change. I never went in there. It was a Saturday morning so he was still in bed and he looked up at me from his pillow. I just stood there frozen. I couldn't talk or move. I just stood there looking at him until tears started to well up in my eyes.

"Come sit next to me, baby girl." He patted the bed beside him. "What is going on?" He was so concerned. I wanted to tell him but I was too ashamed to talk about it. I wasn't sure that I could even get the words out. What would Jason think of me now? I shook my head and started to cry. He put his arms around me and I flinched, but I let him keep holding onto me. After a long time of sobbing like an idiot, I finally was able to get out a couple of sentences.

"Last night," I started, "we didn't go out."

"Oh, I am sorry honey. I had some business to attend to." He sounded so grown up and I felt like some stupid little kid but then something strange happened. He looked at me as if he knew exactly what I was going to say. His face started to turn red. I had said nothing and Jason was sitting there like he knew everything. I started to breathe hard and my eyes began tearing up again.

"Ok, just breathe," he said taking my hand. We sat there in silence for a while until he stood up dragging me with him.

We went to the lake and sat on that tiny bridge. I still hadn't said anything about the night before but I was shaking so he handed me his pocket flask. That was always his answer for everything and it was becoming mine as well.

"Do you see across the lake over there?" He pointed.

"Yea." I stared straight ahead to where he was pointing. I sat there feeling numb inside. I had been broken somehow.

"That is where I am going," he said looking at me. I could feel the electricity in his hand as he brushed my hair from my face. I felt his hand keep ahold of the back of my neck. My entire body was tickled and then he pulled me in. He touched his lips to mine. I didn't move at first and then I kissed him back. I found myself grabbing his shoulders toward me as if that would make him stay longer. It was my first kiss. The foster father had not kissed me on the mouth and I was at least grateful for that. When we pulled away, we kept holding on to each other. It was a mutual feeling of not wanting to let go. Then, he dropped his hands and so did I. We held hands for a while looking at each other.

"You can sleep in my bed tonight," he said. He was reassuring me, but why? I still hadn't told him what had happened. Then, right on queue.

"But . . ." He put his hand to my mouth to stop me.

"Did he touch you, Lily?" He sounded on edge but not so angry. I lowered my head feeling so embarrassed. He grabbed my face and looked me in the eye. All I could do was nod my head yes and tears sprung from my eyes, then he pulled me in closer and hugged me. "Shhh, I'm here. You are safe." And so, I slept in Jason's bed that night.

He held me in his arms as I stared at his walls. I could feel him breathing against my back. Jason's room was blue and he loved the Beatles. He had posters up everywhere. I fell asleep and woke up late. It was Sunday morning and so I didn't move. I still had that gross feeling in the pit of my stomach. Jason stood up in these green and black plaid sweat pants and no shirt. When had he taken his shirt off?

He was perfect. I could see every muscle in his back completely defined. His physique was skinny but I never knew that there were those muscles underneath the shirt. He turned around and saw me staring at him. He looked down at the floor almost as if he was embarrassed. It was kind of cute. He came back to bed and laid beside me. He started to grab me closer when I winced.

"What is it?" He looked concerned.

"Nothing." I tugged at my shirt.

"Let me see." He sounded sad. I lifted my shirt and there was a bruise on my side from where I was held down. The bruise was so pronounced now. It felt worse than it had yesterday. His breathing started to get shallow and I had never seen him look angry before. I pulled my shirt down quickly.

"I have to do something," he said quietly to himself.

"Can I ask you something?" I asked looking at him. "Did you know that this would happen to me?"

"I was hoping it wouldn't," he said, running his hand through his hair and letting out deep breaths. "I did have an idea though, yes."

"Why?" I wasn't sure what I was really asking. Why was this happening to me? Or why did he know this would happen and not warn me? My head was spinning.

"It was his daughter." Jason grabbed my face in his hands looking into my eyes. "What happened to that girl was horrible." He looked sad again. "But she was not my Lily." Tears came to my eyes and he hugged me into his chest. "I am trying to protect you. I promise you I am," he whispered to me, but I wasn't sure that he could. He already hadn't. This horrific thing had already happened to me and I did not want it to happen again.

For at least a good week, I spent the night in Jason's room. I always waited until Ruby fell asleep so I could sneak in there and then sneak back in the morning. I spent every night in his arms talking until I fell asleep. We would talk about everything and nothing and all the little things in between.

"Are you afraid to die?" he asked me one night. The question surprised me. We never really spoke of my condition. We certainly did not talk about me dying.

"I didn't use to be," I said.

"And now you are?" he asked. It was dark and all I could hear was us breathing in sync. I had to think for a minute. Was I afraid to die? Maybe I just had something or someone to live for now.

"No," I answered. Then I felt for the first time in my life that I could say anything that I was thinking, anything at all. "Truth?" I asked.

"Truth," he answered back.

"I am not afraid of dying and I don't think I ever was. There was a time I would have welcomed it, but now I am only afraid of leaving you," I said and then waited for him to say something.

"Of course, you are because I'm awesome." He squeezed me.

"You are a dork." I rolled my eyes and laughed. "I was being serious!"

"So was I!" He laughed.

"I hate you!" I pushed on his chest.

"No, you do not," he said so confidently. Sometimes, he drove me absolutely crazy! But I wouldn't give him up for the world!

"How about you, Mr. Confident, are you afraid of dying?"

"I have never really thought about it before," he answered.

"Everyone has thought about death," I fired back.

"Not me." I could hear the smile in his voice. "Death is inevitable." Then he kissed the back of my neck and sent a tingle down my spine. We had not done anything except kiss so every time he touched me, my body would jump and he would laugh.

I did believe his answer, though. I could believe that Jason really had never thought about dying. He thought about a lot of things, but I don't think I heard him say anything about things that were out of his control. I wished I had his strength.

"Go to sleep," he whispered in my ear. I jumped and he laughed.

"Hey." I shook him awake. "It's late!" I ran out of the room. To my amazement, there was my foster father standing in the hallway. He took one look at me and walked downstairs. I went into my room feeling stunned and scared. Ruby was already awake and dressed.

"Baby girl." Jason poked his head in and threw me a pair of flannel pants.

"What is this?" I asked holding them up. "You love these."

"Yes, I do. However, you never bought sweats to wear. I don't want you to get cold at night." He gave me a meaningful look.

"Breakfast!" the ring of my foster mother's voice trailed up the stairs. Ruby went running down the stairs.

"Coming!" we both answered at once. We looked at each other and started to laugh.

"Put those on now." He stood there waiting.

"Now? Turn around!" I scolded him. Ruby had already run down to the kitchen so we were both standing there alone.

"Lily, you are my best friend. Plus, you have been sleeping in my bed with no pants on for a week!" he said, turning his back to me and then turning back around. "Are your pants on now?" I loved his sarcasm. I loved the way he ignored my wishes as if he was defying the world all of the time.

"They look perfect on you," he smiled. Even though he was a few inches taller than me, I still had to get on my tiptoes to hug or kiss him.

He took me up in his arms and gave me a quick kiss. That was something that I could definitely get used to. He was right though. He was my only friend.

"Best friend, huh?" I put my hands on my hips.

"You are being such a girl right now." He squeezed me again and we headed down to the kitchen.

We sat down in the kitchen around the island to eat a beautiful meal that she prepared. Ruby was shoveling scrambled eggs into her mouth. My hand was starting to shake and Jason took it under the table. I wasn't sure if it was the alcohol or if I was scared of Mark who was standing two feet away from me.

"Dawn, honey," Mark called across the kitchen. She never acknowledged him and he barely spoke to her. Was that why he did what he did or was it the other way around? Was she disgusted with him?

"Hmmm?" she did not seem to feel the need to face him.

Ruby was finishing up breakfast. Mark looked at her and then back up at Dawn.

"Hey, Ruby, why don't you go play with your dolls?" I picked up quickly that it wasn't a conversation that Ruby should be hearing.

"Dawn!" he raised his voice a little.

"Yes, dear?" she smiled but sounded annoyed.

"I saw Lily coming out of Jason's room this morning." He looked at me and then at Jason who was not looking too happy at that instance. "Do you think that is appropriate?"

Dawn looked at us. The one person she did not look at was Mark. Her face said it all and it was almost like her eyes were pleading with Jason not to start any problems. Jason just squeezed my hand under the table. Was that why Jason was sitting on my bed the first day I arrived? Were those Ruby's bad dreams? Just watching the scene, some things started to make sense to me.

"Dawn?" Mark questioned her. Dawn cleared her throat, turned to look at him, and then back at us.

"Jason. Lily . . ." she started, "you two should not get intimate. Especially in this house. Ruby will get confused and Lily, you are too young to be doing anything!"

Suddenly, I was young. My anger rose up in me fast. She knew! How many other girls had suffered? So, my next reaction *was* childish.

"I am *fifteen*! We are *not* even having sex! But ok, I will stay in my bed." I looked at Mark and then walked out the front door. I walked directly to Jason's car and got in slamming the door. He came out and got into the driver's seat.

"So, you are hiding in my car?" He sounded angry but it wasn't directed at me.

"If you are so worried about it, don't leave your doors unlocked," I snapped, looking straight ahead.

"Wear the flannels."

"Because flannels are going to stop him!" my voice rose. I regretted that immediately.

"I'm sorry," I said softly.

His face was red and I could tell he was trying to keep himself from exploding. I took a deep breath while I kept staring out the window. We were there together and that was all that mattered. I reached for his hand and he took mine. He was my angel and he didn't even know it. I looked over at him, but he wasn't looking at me. He was just sitting there fuming. Right, we weren't talking because he felt like he had no way of stopping this. Jason was powerless right now, and so, we sat there in silence.

I felt like I could never look at that woman again. I knew that she knew what was going on. I couldn't think of anything worse than knowing something was going on and not doing anything about it. The thoughts kept running through my head for a good ten minutes. Then, he started the car. We drove around in silence for a very long time. Well, it was a couple of hours at least. He didn't take me to the bridge, which was surprising. We didn't go anywhere. We just didn't go back and even when we got back, he parked on the street and we just sat there.

"What about Ruby?" I finally broke the silence.

"Did you start a conversation in your head that you would like to let me in on?" he looked at me.

"I thought I just did." I raised an eyebrow and got a tiny smile out of him.

"No." He shook his head. "Ruby is safe. Well, as safe as she can be."

"I'm afraid that she saw and heard everything." I looked out the window at all the beautiful cookie-cutter houses.

"She does," he answered in a sad tone. He sounded like he was just as upset about Ruby as I was but he was completely powerless over it. Jason hated being out of control. He hated when he couldn't fix something. He always wanted to fix everything.

"Do you know what is in exactly two weeks from today?" I asked, looking at him almost with tears in my eyes.

"Are you counting the days, sweet girl?" He put his finger under my chin.

"So, what if I am?" I shrugged. It was his birthday and he would be free. I had never felt more terrified in my life.

I wore the flannel pants that night but only because they made me feel closer to Jason. I was just about to fall asleep when I heard the door open and the smell of alcohol was in the air. It didn't smell like the whiskey that we drank but different, more potent even. I looked over at Ruby to see that she was ok and asleep.

He was disgusting as he pulled my blanket back and got into my bed. I usually wore only a nightshirt but tonight was different and it didn't go unnoticed. He yanked the pants off forcefully.

"You want to be with this boy?" he asked. He covered my mouth with one hand and started to hit me with something against my thighs. I didn't know what it was but it hurt. Tears streamed down my face while he held me down and forced himself inside of me. I closed my eyes and waited for it to be over. When he was finished, he left the room and I was literally torn apart. I had been a virgin still and now I was nothing. That's how I felt. I looked down and there was blood everywhere and to make matters even worse, I saw Ruby get up out of the corner of my eye.

"Lily," she called.

"Shh, shh. Everything is ok. Go back to sleep, sweetie, ok?" I kissed the top of her head and went back to her bed. I heard the door to the master bedroom close. I was hysterically crying and screaming inside!

Then, Jason was there gently lifting me up, and he quietly brought me to the bathroom. He washed all the blood off of my thighs and he even went to get another pair of his sweat pants that might fit me. He knew that I could not put jeans on right now. I tried to breathe and stop crying but I couldn't. Once I was all cleaned up, he scooped me up and carried me out the door. When we were outside, I started to get hysterical.

"I never . . ." I sucked in a sob.

"Ok, baby girl. I need you to be quiet right now, ok?" And so, I did as I was told putting both hands over my mouth to stop the screams that wanted to escape from deep within me. He carried me to the park and we laid on the grass that night.

"I was a virgin! It hurt and he hit me. Ruby woke up!" I sobbed. Jason turned on his stomach to kiss me. "Who will want me now?" I did not know what had just happened only that it was horrifying.

"Me." He kissed me again and then I grabbed the bottle from him. He let me drink the entire bottle that night and I woke up in his bed the next morning. I woke up in the morning I went into my room and my sheets were still stained with blood. I put the comforter over it as Ruby woke up for school. Jason didn't take me to school that day. We just sat by the lake on the bridge and drank until I felt numb.

"I am going to get you out of here, honey." He kissed my hand. "I promise." Jason never went around making promises. He was too smart for that. However, he was probably the sweetest and most caring person that I had ever known.

"When?" The question just came out. When I said it, I thought I sounded mean. That didn't matter. Everyone was used to me being mean.

"You are drunk," he said looking at me. He was calling me on how rude I just sounded. That was my Jason always calling me out. He knew the bitter anger was a front to protect myself and at that moment, I felt like I needed to protect myself against everyone and everything.

"I know," I said in a very monotone voice. He looked at me with tears in his eyes. Those were the first tears I had ever seen in those beautiful blue eyes. It made me feel even sadder if that was possible. I scooted closer to him and put my head on his shoulder.

When we finally went back to the house, it was getting dark out. I reluctantly got out of the car. He grabbed me, stopping me from going any farther. I faced him and looked into those eyes. People say that the eyes go straight to the soul or that they see something special when they look into your eyes. When I looked into Jason's eyes, I saw something that I have never seen before. I saw love, the ocean, something completely pure, and I could look into those eyes for the rest of my life.

"What?" I asked as I snapped out of my little trance.

"I am right here with you no matter what." He hugged me close to him for a long time and then we walked into the house together. No one was downstairs that we could see but the hall light was on. That was weird because it was only like 9 p.m. We walked up the stairs together, still no sign of anyone. We stood in the hallway between our rooms. I peeked in my room and saw Ruby under the glow of her night light. Still, no sign of the foster parents.

"Does this seem weird to you?" I asked furrowing my eyebrows.

"Hopefully, Mark is passed out drunk somewhere." I knew that he was trying to sound hopeful for me. I would have made him stay up a little longer with me but I was buzzed and I felt like lying down anyway. So, I stood on my tiptoes and gave him a long passionate kiss. His hands were in my hair and I wished I could stay in that moment forever. I didn't want to let go of him. He made me feel safe and I was beginning to feel my body wanting him. I touched his chest. He felt so strong. He looked simply amazing to me and all I wanted was to go into his room and touch every part of him. But when he squeezed me in closer to him, I flinched.

"What's wrong?" He almost looked afraid. I didn't respond. Instead, I began to cry like a child. Then, he pulled me in again and I put my head on his chest. "Shhh, baby girl. Everything is going to be ok," he whispered in my ear. "*You* are going to be ok." We stood in the hallway like that until I calmed down. He put his finger under my chin bending down to kiss me.

"Are you sure that you don't want to sleep in my bed tonight?" All I could do was shake my head no. I almost felt angry with him. Why wasn't he getting me out of here? How was any of this going to be ok?

"I do not want to repeat Mark's anger," I said more worried about Ruby than anyone. She was so little. I hated that she had to witness any of this at all.

"Ok," he hesitated. "You sure?"

"I am fine, kid. I am fine," I said as I wiped tears from my eyes and tried to put on a fake smile. Of course, he didn't believe me, but he was the last person who dared tell me what to do. We both walked into our separate bedrooms. I closed the door as quietly as I could and sat on my bed. Then I reached underneath my bed and grabbed my bottle of whiskey I had hidden there. I smiled to myself. At least, I had this and I took a few swigs. The next thing I knew, I heard someone outside the door of our room. I stood up with the bottle ready for anything, then there was a click and footsteps walking away.

I walked slowly over to the door and grabbed the handle. It was locked. It was locked! My heart started to race as I examined the handle. They had reversed the lock on the doorknob. I went to the window and it was the same thing. I couldn't stop thinking logically. I just sank to my knees, my heart racing. My chest was hurting and I was panicking! There was no one there to help. All of a sudden, I did not care about waking Ruby. I just screamed.

"Jason!" It was more of a shriek really, but I heard him calling my name. I thought that I heard him outside of my door and then everything started going black. When I opened my eyes, all I saw was a man with amazing green eyes and a smile that could kill. I looked up at him and then around the room that was now empty. There were no beds, no Ruby, just he and I on the floor. He was kneeling next to me. My heart rate was still rapid and my breathing was getting too shallow. Was this really happening? I had no idea what was going on. Was I dying?

"Lily," he started, "look at me, baby girl." My chest hurt and I looked around the room again. "Lily. I need you to focus on me. I need you to breathe." He almost sounded exactly like Jason. Maybe I was dreaming and it really was Jason. Nevertheless, I looked into those oddly familiar green eyes and began to breathe. Everything slowed down, everything! My breathing, my heart rate, even time, seemed to be still.

"Are you feeling a little better now?" he asked. I saw tears in his eyes. I nodded. "Lily, I am here. You are never alone, baby girl." He put his hand on my head. Why was he calling me that? No one but Jason called me that and was this even real? It felt real. Then I opened my eyes and all I heard was screaming. I sat up and looked around the room again. The screaming was coming from outside of the room. I spotted Ruby in the corner of the room on the floor curled up in a ball and crawled over to her.

"Are you ok, honey?" I was trying to stay calm but my head was spinning. Was I hallucinating? That didn't matter right now. I was trying to listen to who was yelling outside of the door. I thought it was the foster dad and mom, but it was Jason. He was screaming at the foster mother. I did not hear the foster father out there at all.

"Please, Jason," she was pleading with him.

"Do you know how sick she is?"

"I don't have the key." She sounded small and helpless. "Ruby is in there. Don't you think I want to get in there too?"

"Fine!" Apparently, they had been fighting about calling the police. I heard a huge bang and then crack. I looked up and there he was, rushing to my side. That's my boy. I smiled to myself. Ruby got up and ran out of the room to the foster mother. Jason grabbed me onto his lap. Our faces were touching but I was still crying. I felt safe now, but I had already felt safe when I woke up from that dream or whatever that was. Something had happened. I mean I know I fainted but what was that? Did I have a brain tumor now too? The last thing I needed was to die when I found my soul mate—the one person who I could be *me* with. I was always safe and never judged.

"Are you ok? Does your chest hurt?" He nuzzled me. "I am so sorry, Lily!" I thought he was about to cry. Lily? He never called me Lily. He must have been extremely upset. Of course, he was! I was locked in a room with *Ruby* and for what? Did he just want to keep Jason out?

"Well, I am ok now," I said in a monotone voice. Then, he lifted me up and we walked past the foster mother who was hugging Ruby and out the front door. We got in his car and started driving. We were always driving those days. It was just too bad it wasn't away from there, not yet anyway.

"*What* happened?" I turned on him. He could smell the whiskey on my breath. I could tell because he squinted at me, but no judgment, so nothing was said. He had suggested once that I stop drinking so much and I guess the look I gave him was enough to stop that. He was probably right but with everything going on, I just wanted to *not* feel once in a while.

"Apparently, Mark decided that he was going to lock you in a room from now on." He was so angry I could almost feel the heat coming off of him.

"Where was he then?" I asked just as angrily. "He locked me up so he could just . . ." I couldn't say the words. "Then he just disappeared?" I was so confused.

"No, he was there. I think it was my knife." He smiled finally. He pulled out his prize pocket knife. It was small enough to fit in his pocket yet big enough to look scary and I started to laugh. Then, we both laughed hysterically until we hurt. That felt good. We needed a laugh even if it was over something horrible.

"You have a bat too, you know." I pointed at him and raised my eyebrow.

"Yes, baby girl, I know." He smiled at me. "Last resort," he said, glaring playfully at me.

"And this was not the last resort?" I folded my arms and looked out the window. "Can I ask where you are taking us?"

"Where do you want to go?" Jason never held a grudge, well at least not with me. He bounced back so quickly that I wish I was more like him.

"Take me to the bridge." That bridge had become *our* place and my hope—the hope that Jason would take me with him when he left. I could not imagine a life without him in it.

When we arrived, he parked the car right off the road, and then we walked over to the bridge and sat side by side like we always did. The night air was cool and felt good in my lungs. I took deep breaths.

"Are you feeling alright?" he asked when he saw me breathing.

"No, I am not alright. But my lungs are fine. I am just taking in the night air."

"Yes, I am sure that you are shaken up."

"Well, that is the understatement of the year," I snapped a little. "I'm sorry."

"You never have to apologize to me, baby girl." He put his head on my shoulder for once. His heart was beating so hard and so fast that I could not even feel my own.

"Show me again," I said smiling with hope. So, he pointed over to the other side of the bridge and past all the trees that were acting as a barrier. I could not see past them, but I knew it was there, wherever *there* was. "Is it Washington?" I asked.

"No. It is just over the border in Oregon."

"So, it is *really way* over there!" I exclaimed and he nudged me playfully. "Do you know why I come here?" he asked thoughtfully.

"Hmm?" I was lost in my thoughts about the "dream" that I had.

"Because to get to where I am going to live, there is a bridge exactly like this little bridge with a sign welcoming you into this small town." He pointed beyond the trees. "That is where I'm going." Then I snapped.

"*You? You are going*?" Now I had started yelling. "Why do we stay there? Why don't you get us out?" Tears started rolling down my cheeks partly because I was angry and partly because I felt bad that I was yelling at him. I could yell at anyone, but I did not usually yell at Jason. He just looked at me for a minute stunned.

"I would leave right now if I could! You know that I have to wait the two weeks until my birthday, you know I have to wait for the money, and why on earth do you think I would *ever* leave you behind!" he yelled back. He had never yelled at me before. Now, it was my turn to be stunned. He gathered himself and then tried to touch my arm but I flinched away. "I'm sorry," he said softly. "I am just frustrated."

"You are frustrated?" I pronounced each word with a good deal of sarcasm.

Again, I was not so nice. Why was I doing this to him? Why was I being so mean to the one person in the world who I loved? I hung my head down. I was exhausted and my whole body felt irritated. He looked straight ahead at the other side of the bridge. I laid my head on his shoulder and closed my eyes.

"Ok, can we stop fighting with each other and think of something constructive?" He asked for my comfortable silence. I was enjoying it.

"Always the logical one." I looked up forcing a tiny smile.

"Lily, I am so serious. You are all I have in this world. I can't lose you, not ever! That is why I didn't call the police . . ." he trailed off.

"Because they would have taken me away," I finished the thought.

"I was so scared, baby girl." He looked so sad it broke my heart. "I can't let anything happen to you." He grabbed my hand and squeezed it, but he looked as though he was holding something back.

"Ok!" I exclaimed. "We are being constructive, right? And by *we,* I mean *you*." I and he rolled his eyes but he knew that it was true. I was emotional and he was logical. That was how our relationship worked. At least, I thought it was a relationship.

"Man." He shook his head. "You sure know how to ruin a moment." I looked at him completely confused.

"What?" I looked surprised at him. He grabbed me under my arms helping me down off the railing that I probably shouldn't have been sitting on in the first place and then it happened. He cupped his hands around my face. His hands were shaking and I remember thinking that was weird.

"Lily," he started, "I am in love with you. You just 'happened' to me one day. I didn't see you coming but I'm so glad you did. I wasn't even looking for you. I do not want you to worry that I am going to leave you behind. I will never leave you behind." I looked into his eyes and saw everything pure. I didn't deserve this kind of love, did I? I was about to tell him how I felt when we saw headlights coming up the road. He grabbed my hand ducking us back to his car in the dark. Then the moment had passed, so I had to decide to let it go.

"Hey." We got into the car. "We still haven't decided on what we are going to do."

"Well." I could practically hear him thinking. His wheels turned so fast when he was thinking. I loved watching him think; it was almost beautiful. "Stop it." He turned to look at me.

"What are you talking about?" I asked, looking at him mischievously.

"You know what you are doing." I squinted my eyes at him.

"Nope, I still can't hear what you came up with in all that thinking going on." I smiled. The silver lining was that even with all of the hell that we were living through, we could still make each other smile.

"We have to get out of there." He looked so focused and he was biting his lip, just like when he was somewhere in his head. It wasn't what he *did* tell me that evening. It was what he didn't tell me!

"I have a friend." He turned to look at me as he got excited. "I need to call him and see if the loft can be ready early."

A loft? That was the first time I heard about that. I wanted to ask about it but all of a sudden, my chest and my head were hurting.

I grabbed my head whining about the pain. It felt like my head was being crushed and it was light as if I was floating. This was new. What was happening? I wasn't in pain anymore. Jason and the car were gone. I was somewhere else and I could see and hear clearly.

"It is not time yet!" I could see a very pretty blonde talking to someone but who? Who was she talking to? I could feel a presence. It made me feel like crying. Then, my chest pain and my head felt fine again. I was back in the car with my boy again.

"What happened?" Jason's hand was resting on my head that was resting on the back of the seat.

"I don't know." Should I tell him? "I have no idea!" I must have been freaking out because he took both of my hands in his. "All of a sudden, I was in a lot of pain and then it just went away." *Nice one telling him the truth, Lily*, I thought to myself. I couldn't tell him. I couldn't tell *anyone* because I needed to know what was happening to me first. They would think I was going crazy and why wouldn't they? I thought I was going crazy!

"Are you sure, baby girl? Because you look like you just saw a ghost." Maybe I had.

"I am fine, really. Stop being so overprotective!" I quipped, forcing a smile at him. "So, is there a rest of this plan?"

"We hope my friend says yes?" He said, shrugging his shoulders.

"What are we going to do until then, Jay?" I panicked. I didn't want to have to go back there ever. Then, he said something completely unexpected.

"We find the key."

"We will get out of there as soon as we can. Just let me make the call." He pulled out his cellphone and dialed. "Voicemail," he whispered to me. "Hey Ian, it's Jason. I have an urgent situation and I need to speak with you asap! Please call me back." He sounded insanely desperate. But that name, Ian? Why was that so familiar to me? Better yet, why was I feeling sick to my stomach when things sound familiar? A normal person would have thought it sounded familiar and went on with their lives, but not me! Do I need to have weird feelings and visions? What was happening? It all started when I came to live at this horrible house, and yet, I cannot say it was completely horrible because it brought me to Jason.

CHAPTER SIX

As stupid as it was, we went back to the house and that night, the foster father came in and whipped me with a belt all over my thighs, butt, and arms. Was he not even trying to hide it? That night, he had sex with me again. I laid there waiting for it to be over. When he left the room, I turned over and screamed into my pillow. I no longer cared about Ruby or Jason or anything! I sobbed into my pillow and there was nobody in the world who could have helped me that night.

I felt Jason in the doorway. I didn't look up. I did not want him to come in. I was physically in so much pain! My emotional status was ripped to shreds, so I stayed in my pillow where it was safe for that moment. Jason stood in my doorway for as long as I was awake that night.

When I woke up the next day, Ruby was nowhere to be seen. The foster mother had not woken me up and it was a school day. Everything was unusually quiet but I welcomed it. As I was sitting up, I felt my entire body hurt. I looked down at my thighs. They weren't only bruised but sliced and bleeding. My butt was killing me! I didn't even look at my arms. I could feel them too. When I worked up the courage to stand, I looked at my sheets that were covered in blood and white stuff that I knew was semen. I almost threw up so I got to the bathroom as soon as I could.

I started the warm water and got into the shower, but I had to back out of it because the cuts stung. I was standing there crying when Jason walked in. I pulled back the shower curtain and was grateful that at least, it was him. He looked so sad and concerned. How could he possibly want me now?

"What are you doing?" I asked.

"I want to see if you're hurt," he demanded, "and you are *my* beautiful girl. Stop being self-conscious." I glared at him. The one thing about Jason was that even though he was so sweet, his tone was always so serious. It was something that I had gotten used to and it actually brought me some comfort. It was like every little thing actually mattered to him.

"I am," I said, curtly closing the shower curtain. I loved the way that Jason never put up with my crap, although I could tell that he was being extremely gentle with me.

"Only your hands are in the water," he said, pulling the curtain back open. Then, there it was, the look. He looked at how bad it was and I think that he was in shock. I went to grab my towel and he stopped me.

"Lily, you are *my* beautiful girl. I have seen you naked before so cut it out," he said with a serious tone again and then he kissed me softly on the lips. I wanted to tell him that I loved him and that I felt completely ruined for him now but the words were just stuck in my throat. Instead, I started crying. I think that he was looking me over. If he was angry, he didn't show it.

"I still haven't showered," I said through my tears. There was a sadness that even I could hear in my voice. Jason held up a tube of cream and gauze.

"They don't want anyone to see my arms. That's why no one woke me up." I said out loud, not really directed at anyone. He started taking care of all of my cuts on my butt and thighs. Even my arms were all bandaged up.

"Come on," I said still, sitting on the toilet. "Will you please grab me a clean shirt?" I asked as nicely as I could. He left the bathroom and came back with one of his t-shirts and a pair of gray flannel pants. It was perfect, I thought to myself.

"What are we doing?" I asked as I tried to get up. He finally just grabbed me under my arms. "Whoa there, are you okay?"

"I'm fine." I looked at him, determined. He did not question me after that. "Really, I'm ok, I'm just hurt, that's all," I said it so casually as if I hadn't been beaten just the night before and forced to sleep in my own blood. He let go of me and let me limp a few steps forward. "See?" I looked back at him. "Now, come on."

"What are we doing?" It was Jason's turn to follow.

"We are going to find that key and whatever else he might have." I'm not sure why I said that. Why would I think that he had something else hidden away? Jason followed me into the master bedroom. I looked around the room wondering where to start. Jason took my lead without question and we went through all of the dressers and cabinets. We even looked under the bed.

After about half an hour in the master bedroom, we were ready to start looking at other places in the house when I saw it. How did we not see it before? We had been looking and rummaging and the whole time, it was right in front of us. In the far corner of the room was a bookshelf. Why would I not notice a book that looked so out of place in the room? Jason was halfway out of the door when he turned back to me.

"Come on." He nodded to the hallway.

"Jason," I said his name softly and slowly, "did you look at the bookshelf?"

"No, I thought you did. What's up, baby girl?" He looked at me curiously. I walked closer to the bookcase.

"Is that a book?" I pointed as I walk closer. There was something light gray that almost looked like a book. Almost. I went over and touched it. It had been out of my eyesight and I thought we had rummaged through all of the books. I lifted my hand and tried to grab it. It was cold and hard. I winced back down immediately. My arms were not in the best shape. Jason who was taller than me by a few inches reached up and grabbed it, taking it down off of the shelf.

It was not a book. It was not even something useless. It was a case. We set it down on the floor. It had a black handle and a lock. Really? What could possibly be in there and what was it?

"It's a fire-safe box." Jason piped up out of nowhere. I furrowed my eyebrows looking at the lock.

"What could possibly be in there?" I asked, still focusing on the box.

"Well," Jason started, "it is big enough for a key and people usually use these things to protect important documents or money in case of a fire. You never know with Mark." He was looking intently at me like he was waiting for me to do something.

"It's locked." I looked up at him. I had been staring at the keyhole this entire time. Both of us were sitting on the floor of the master bedroom with something that we obviously shouldn't have and we didn't care who walked in on us. That was the furthest thought from my mind. I wanted to get in that box. The key to every room in this house could be in there. *There could be money*, I thought to myself, *we could definitely use that when we got out of here*. Then, Jason gave me his little mischievous smile.

"I think I know where it is." He stood up.

"Seriously?" He gave me his hand and I stood up. "How would you just know that?" I looked at him suspiciously.

"You would think that by you would trust." He cocked his head to the side.

"Fine." I rolled my eyes. I still was not confident that he knew what he was doing, but it couldn't hurt.

"We are just going to leave it here?" I asked in almost a whisper.

"Yes, this will just take a minute and if I'm wrong, we come and put it back." I started toward the stairs. I did not want to put it back! I wanted to get in there and find that key and whatever else these horrible people might be hiding.

He walked behind me down the stairs as I slowly and painfully made my way down. Then, he took the lead and we headed toward the dining room. We stopped in a small room between the kitchen and in the dining room where there was a good-sized wet bar where we stole all of our alcohol from. On the very top shelf, there were all of the foster father's expensive bottles. Jason reached, took one of the bottles down, and set it on the marble countertop. Then, he reached up again, taking down the bottle behind it. Both of the bottles were full.

"Tequila." He gave me a sly grin. "See you, baby girl." He started as he opened the bottle. "Some tequilas have a worm at the bottom." He took the bottle and poured it into the sink right down to the last drop until I heard a small clink hitting the stainless-steel sink. "This bottle has a key at the bottom." He held up a small metal key that looked like it might fit the lock.

"How did you . . ." I trailed off looking at my darling smart boy in amazement.

"Don't look so surprised." He gave me a dirty look. "Don't you know by that I know a lot of things?" I cocked my head and looked back at him. It didn't smell like alcohol. I watched as he filled the bottle back up with water and replaced both bottles.

"Water?" I asked.

"Yup." He held the key and started back through the kitchen again. My stomach had butterflies! Was this the key?

When we returned, we sat back down next to the safe.

"Do you want to do the honors?" he asked, handing me the key.

"Yes, I do." I took the key from him and then slowly tried to insert it into the keyhole. I heard it click and then it snapped open. What I saw was unexpected. Not only was there no key or money but there I was.

"The . . ." I grabbed a piece of paper out of the box. It was my birth certificate. There was no name or signature but it was my birth date and it was definitely a birth certificate. Then, there were pictures of me over the last few years, the social work papers on my different foster homes, and my medical records. “What is this?” I started to feel like I was going to throw up. My chest started to hurt.

“Ok, baby girl, just breathe.” Easy for him to say. He wasn’t the one who was being stalked and why? I watched as he looked through all of the papers and pictures and then he held something else up. It looked like more medical records. “Ruby,” he said quietly.

“What is this?” I stood up and the pain didn’t matter. I was very confused and very angry. Who were these people? Jason stood up with me. He went to put his hands on my arms and then stopped short, realizing the pain I was in. At this point, the pain was obsolete.

“Ruby is sick.” He was calculating and calm.

“Ruby? What does Ruby have to do with this? With me?” I started sweating I couldn’t tell if the room was hot or I was just so upset. Then, he handed me a piece of paper. “What is this?” I asked, handing it back to him.

“It’s a DNA test.” He still held my stare. I still had no idea what all of this meant.

“Why do they have all of this information on me, Jason?” I demanded. At first, he said nothing. It looked as though he didn’t want to answer my question. At the same time, he looked just as confused as I was.

“This test says that Ruby is your biological sister.” He was still holding the paper in his hands.

“What?” My forehead began to sweat and I started to feel faint. “Is that possible? Why is my birth certificate in here?” I wanted to sound angry but it came out weak. Then, I realized what was happening. I ran into the hall and into the bathroom just in time to throw up in the sink. Jason was right behind me.

There was a ringing in my ears at first and then pain seared into my head. I squeezed my eyes shut but I could still see him clearly. I saw dark eyes and sadness there. He put his hands down. Just when I felt the pain subsiding, I heard his voice clear and deep. Then, I heard my name. “Lily, girl.”

I was squatting on the bathroom floor with my head in my own hands when I finally opened my eyes. What was happening? I was falling apart and losing my mind! I started to cry right there on the bathroom floor.

"Hey," Jason said in a soft voice sitting next to me.

"I'm losing it, Jay." I shook my head and sobbed.

"No, you are not." He sounded tough and confident. Why was he so confident in me? I felt small and weak. What had this world ever done for me but leave me behind and cause excruciating pain? I didn't tell him what I was experiencing. I couldn't tell him. We had enough to deal with. Me losing my mind was not one of them.

CHAPTER SEVEN

When I felt somewhat back to normal, I tried to stand up from the bathroom floor. I was dizzy halfway up. Jason grabbed me as lightly as he could and took me to my room.

"I'm fine." I insisted.

"No, you are not fine. You are everything but fine!" He was getting upset now.

"Did you know about this?" I asked. I tried to sound nice but it came out more accusatory.

"No," he answered calmly looking into my eyes. I laid back on my bed and then a thought came to me.

"Are they my parents?" I asked, disgusted with the thought. Jason was still standing there next to my bed.

"I don't know." Then, he just walked out of my room without another word. No doubt, he was going to put everything back the way it was. But how was I going to get answers? What was wrong with Ruby and why did they come looking for me? Was the foster mother really my biological mother who I had hated all of these years?

I laid in bed the rest of the afternoon with my mind spinning and anger surging in and out of my body. Jason did not come back in after he cleaned up, but I did hear his car leave. I wondered where he was going for a second and then I didn't care again. I was back to not caring because not caring didn't hurt so badly as being lied to.

"Lily?" It was Ruby. She had been in the room the whole time that I was being beaten. The poor baby and her mother did nothing. She looked so sweet with her red hair pulled back in a ponytail with a black bow on top.

"Ruby." I sat up slowly. "Hi, sweetheart." I already adored this little girl but knowing now that she was my little sister made me care even more.

"Are you ok?" she asked, looking down at her feet.

"Come sit up here with me." I patted the bed and she jumped up next to me. I tried not to cry. The last thing I wanted was for her to see me looking weak. She needed me now and she needed me to be strong for her.

"Do you like Jason?" she asked so innocently. The question surprised me so much that I didn't know what to say.

"Yes. I do like him." I smile at her. I could not just leave her here, but I couldn't stay here either

CHAPTER EIGHT

"We are leaving." And he opened the shower curtain. "*Tomorrow.*" I knew that he had seen all the bruises that were now all over my back. He kissed me hard and long and walked out of the bathroom. He was the only person in the world who really cared about me. Our love was more than a crush. He was my best friend and my family now. He was protecting me.

That night was different. When Mark came in the room, he had a wild, almost determined look on his face. He came onto the bed and then he forced himself in behind me in a different place this time and I screamed! It hurt so badly and I kept screaming. Then, everything went dark.

I woke and Jason was standing over that bastard with a bat. There was blood everywhere, I could not tell whose blood it was.

"Come on, Lily." I heard his voice but I was paralyzed. I might have been crying as well but I definitely could not move. Jason kneeled down on the floor in front of me and pleaded.

"Baby girl, we need to go now!" I looked into his eyes and for a split second, his eyes were green and his calm warmed me. I shook my head and my blue-eyed boy was back. I could see the foster mother standing in the hallway with the phone, but I could tell that she was waiting to call until we left. They couldn't take me away, not away from Jason.

Blood. There was so much blood. Was some of it mine? I was confused but I let Jason pull me to my feet. I was aware of Ruby crying. I was not aware that all I was wearing was a t-shirt with blood on it. Nothing else, shoes or underwear, nothing.

"Ruby," was all I could say.

"She will be ok," he assured me. "We have to go *now,* honey!" His tone was sweet but urgent. I let him drag me out of the house and to the car. He opened the passenger door and made sure I could get in ok. It was hard for me to sit. Everything sounded far away for a couple of minutes while I was still disoriented.

"Lily, Lily?" The ringing in my ears stopped and I could hear him clearly again. I was in pain and confused. "Are you hurt?" he asked.

"Yes." My throat felt tight. "What happened?" I demanded.

"I don't know," he answered. He had a very serious look on his face. His eyes stayed focused on the road while we sped away from the house.

"What do you mean?" I was hysterical and he was so calm.

"What happened in there, baby?" He was sincere.

"I don't know. He was there and then everything went dark." I really had no idea what was going on.

It went dark like when you faint. Was there a difference? I have the answer to that. No, it is not the same. It feels like I did not make the decision. When I drank, I was deciding and this feels like I'm there one moment and just gone the next. When I woke up, I had felt like I was alone. Like it was a dream. Yes, there is a fine line between when I faint and when my world goes dark, but there is one. It felt like it was happening or it did happen. The voices and people are real but I can't quite place them. How could I tell him that? If I can't understand it myself, how could I explain it to Jason? It was not that, everything just went black.

I sat there trying to remember. He looked over at me puzzled.

"What are you doing?" he asked. Obviously, he had never seen *me* thinking hard before.

"I'm trying to remember, but I don't."

"Pain?"

"Yes. Less when I don't move." He rolled his eyes.

"Reach behind you, baby girl." Of course, he had alcohol in the back seat!

"Jason? What did happen? At least, what do you know?" Again, my voice was small and sad. I put the bottle to my lips, closed my eyes, and chugged.

"That bastard," he said under his breath. "You screamed, baby girl. Not just a scream but a blood-curdling scream and you were calling my name. Do you remember any of that?" I shook my head no and took another sip of my special whiskey. "He was on top of you. It looked like he was inside you, so I ran to grab my bat to get him off of you. You were still screaming, then I got him off of you. For me, the rest went red. I kept hitting and hitting until I realized what I was doing. Then, I immediately came to your side and got you out of there."

I felt sick. What had happened? Why didn't I remember it? At some point, my wits came back to me and I realized that I was wearing only a nightshirt and that I had no idea where Jason was going. Did he know? I looked outside into the darkness for a moment before I said anything.

"Where are we going?" I asked, looking at him. He had blood on him too.

"I am taking you somewhere safe." His answers were short and precise. He wasn't taking the time to sugarcoat it for me. Then suddenly, he looked sad. "I should have gotten you out of there sooner. I am so sorry." His voice broke.

"I don't remember any of it so . . ." I trailed off. I was trying to comfort him and I couldn't do it right then.

"I had a plan," he said smiling at me. He grabbed my hand and a sudden calm came over me as it always did when he touched me. "Breathe, baby girl." His voice came in a soft whisper.

I was *freaking out* and he was calm as always. This often frustrated me but tonight, it was particularly hard. I knew he was angry. Why could he not act like it?

We had been driving for about an hour when he stopped at a twenty-four-hour Walmart. "I'm going to get you some clothes," he said. "Will you be ok here for a couple of minutes?" he asked. I nodded. I was terrified but I didn't want him to know that.

When he returned, he came back with a complete outfit, underwear and all. They all fit perfectly of course. I would not have expected anything less from him. He knew everything about me. He was my brain when I couldn't think. I looked at the white sweat pants and matching t-shirt. I looked at the underwear and decided that was not going to happen, not with my butt being so hurt. My butt hurt. Wait!

"I know what happened," I told Jason after getting dressed. I was so ashamed I didn't want to feel any more ruined for him than I already did. He was staring at me with those eyes I could look into. "What?"

"It's you." He looked into my eyes. "I love you. You know that?"

"You had mentioned that once," I whispered. "Jason, I love you too. I mean I don't think that I really know what love is. But if it is the way I feel about you, then *yes* I am in love with you too."

We just sat in the car for a bit, not talking or doing anything. It was like we both just wanted to stay in that moment for just a little while. I never told him what I had remembered that night.

"Are you still in pain?" he asked after the peaceful silence.

"Only when I move," he smiled at me. That was me. The world as we knew it had ended and I was making smart-ass remarks. I laughed with him.

"Your whole body looks bruised." He looked worried and maybe a little sad. Then, he pulled another one of my bottles of whiskey out from behind my seat.

"Where did you—?" I started.

"I grabbed a bunch of things from that sick household." He looked angry. I was positive that he was angry about what had happened. I certainly was. I was traumatized.

I hesitated but then I opened the bottle. I knew it would help the pain. All of the pain. After all, alcohol had become my best friend these last few months, all because one person had touched my life. Before Jason, I was angry and alone, and now, I had a home. Sitting in that car, I realized that. I sat there looking at him so determined to go wherever it was that he was taking me.

"Where are we going?" I asked softly. We had been driving all night and all day.

"I told you. I'm taking you somewhere safe." He smiled that crooked smile that I had come to fall in love with. I knew better than to push him. Jason was someone who commanded respect and trust and I knew better than to question him. So, we kept driving in silence for a long time before he finally broke it again.

"Lily, I have a plan and it is far away from the lives we lived. It's far away from being orphans in Seattle." He paused. "I also didn't think I would have to beat a man to death tonight. So, my plan had to come a little early."

"I know. I was there." He rolled his eyes at me.

"Baby girl, I already had a plan before that. I had an idea I would have to speed it up a bit." Once again, Jason totally disarmed me. I didn't know what had happened that night. I didn't know if people were dead because of me or how Ruby would survive this. I only knew that I was with Jason now and he was my family. I couldn't hide from him and I hated that. He saw right through me always.

"What is wrong?" he asked gently but firmly. I stayed quiet for a moment.

"Ruby," I finally said.

"Ruby?" he asked. "Ruby will be fine. Child services will come and get her out of there."

"How do you know? They are her birth parents. She is my little sister and I don't even know if she is ok." I almost sounded desperate. Ruby, in the few short months that I had known her, had become like a little sister to me. I worried more about her after I found out that she was my biological sister. What if her life turned out like ours? I didn't want that for her. I wouldn't wish that on anyone.

"I will make sure that Ruby is ok. Ok?" He glanced at me. "O-k?"

"Fine, ok." I knew I was sick but I didn't know exactly what was wrong with me or why they came looking for me after fifteen years! What if no one came to take her? What if she wasn't ok? A bad feeling just consumed me at that moment. Not even Jason could understand.

"I promise," he said as if he knew what I was thinking. I nodded. We continued driving without another word about Ruby.

I fell asleep after drinking half the bottle of whiskey. I sat up straighter in the seat just in time to see that we were crossing the state line into Oregon.

"Hey, sunshine," Jason said, "I lost you there for a bit." The sun was setting. Where were we going? Would we be safe finally from the lives we were so fiercely running away from?

"We are almost there," he said sounding excited. Then suddenly, it was there, the bridge—an old wooden bridge. It still looked stable but I was sure that it had been kept up for a long time. It was the bridge. I was almost just as excited as he was.

"We are—" Then an oncoming car came straight for us. And we swerved and then everything went dark. I saw a boy holding onto a little girl's hand. They were laughing and running. "Lily!" Then it was gone. It felt like it had really happened. I don't remember ever seeing this boy.

I woke up cold and wet on a hard surface. As my memory came back quickly, I remembered the car and Jason. I turned my head and there he was, lying on the ground next to the car. There was a man doing CPR on him. I tried to scream but I couldn't make a sound so I crawled over to him.

"No, no, no . . ." I heard the words come out but it was as if someone else was saying them. All I remembered was pain everywhere. He was laying there and was dying. I didn't even look at anyone else. I was crying and my voice was hoarse. "Jason!" I put my head on his chest and listened for the heartbeat that would never come.

"*No*, you can't leave me! *You* are my home and you promised you would never leave me." I laid on his chest sobbing until I felt someone tried to pry me off of him.

"No! He needs to wake up!"

"We need to get him to the hospital so we can help your friend." The EMT was so nice.

"Wait!" I looked at him. I knew that he was already gone. I put my hands on his warm cheeks and kissed him. My tears fell onto his face and I kissed him. I looked into those blue eyes. "You have to stay with me." I backed off then.

The ambulance was there and they took him away. I went with them. How could I leave him? Then, the thought came to me. He left me here all alone. I had nothing and no one. Jason was my love, my best friend, and my home. I was grateful that I was able to lay there with him until they took him away. It was my way of knowing that he was really gone—my head on his chest not hearing and feeling his heart beating. I guess I was lucky. I got to say goodbye. None of these thoughts gave me any comfort. What was I supposed to do now? I had no idea what *the plan* was!

Gone. Jason was gone. That was all I could think the entire ride to the hospital. It felt so surreal. They tried covering his face but I wouldn't let them. I needed to see him for as long as I could. I needed the reality to set in. Or maybe I was waiting for him to wake up.

CHAPTER NINE

"Goodbye, my blue-eyed boy. I will always love you." The tears were rolling down my cheeks and onto his throat. The once lively boy that I knew was gone. We were going to be alone living a happy life together, and now what?

I finally let them put a sheet over him and wheel him away. I closed my eyes and pretended that none of this was happening. How could this happen! We had been so close to a life together—a life where we could be a family. My love was *dead*! There was no car, place, or distance I could use to get to him now. He was really gone.

I sat in the hospital until the doctor came out to tell me what I already knew. Jason was dead. *Dead*. The word *dead* was what made it real for me. I had confirmed wanting him cremated. I had no home or phone number so I asked when and where I could pick up his ashes. I felt like I had been sleepwalking this whole time. Nothing seemed real. I didn't even know where he was planning on taking me.

Then, it finally happened. The reality finally did set in and I felt a pain so deep inside the pit of my stomach that I could barely stand it. The tears came again but this time, I let out a scream, a painful moan and I was sure that everyone was looking but I could not control it. I was lifted by a set of strong arms that took me outside. I was so disoriented I didn't even fight it. He put me down and I slumped against a wall outside of the hospital. I sat there and cried not even knowing what had happened to the car. I had no idea what was going on and my head was spinning. I tried breathing to calm myself down and then I did something that I had never done before. I prayed.

"God, please help me." That was all I could get out. I was still sitting against the wall when I felt a presence next to me. He sat down saying nothing. I looked at him. He had been the arms that had brought me out here. He was staring at me. No way! It was the man giving Jason CPR. He must have seen the shock on my face I am sure but he only smiled at me gently. Immediately, my entire body was calmed and my heart stopped racing.

It was *him*! It was the man in my dreams, the one who could calm me the way Jason had, and the person I had never told anyone about, not even Jason.

"Is there anything I can do?" he asked.

"Can you make my best friend not be dead?" I asked harshly. There she was, the Lily we all know and love. I was filled with anger and bitterness. The only person in this world who loved me through it was gone. *Dead!*

He had green eyes that almost sparkled and skin that was perfect. His dark hair was messy like he had just rolled out of bed. He was not just good-looking. He was strangely beautiful. I could not take my eyes off of him. My chest started to hurt. I wasn't sure if I was in physical pain or emotional.

"Are you ok?" he asked. That was the dumbest question I had ever heard in my life. Of course, I was *not* ok.

"Well," I started, "my best friend and possibly the only person I have ever loved just died. I have nowhere to go and I have no idea where I am. So, no I am not ok." There was an edge in my voice. I just wanted to unleash my anger on everyone and everything. I wished I could say that I felt bad for snapping at this beautiful stranger but I didn't feel bad. All I could do was feel bad for myself. I understand that was not the healthiest thing in the world but I had no idea how else to feel.

Out of the corner of my eye, I saw him smile. That made me angrier! I stood up and turned to leave.

"Wait," he pleaded, standing up with me. "I didn't mean to upset you, Lily."

"Who are you?" I demanded. How on earth did he know my name? "How do you know my name?"

"I know more about you than you can imagine." He quickly shut his mouth as if he had said something wrong.

"How can you see any humor in this?" I asked.

"I don't see any humor in any of this." He looked stunned by me. What did I say that was so horrible? Why was he looking at me like that?

"Then how can you smile at my pain?" He looked confused for a moment and then it seemed to click.

"I smiled." It was a statement as if he was telling himself. "I smiled because you are exactly the person who I thought you would be." We stood there looking at each other. I felt safe and calm. I didn't want him to leave me all of a sudden. I shook the feeling off. There was no way I was getting attached to anyone else ever again. Plus, I felt like I was betraying Jason. Yet, I knew this man. I didn't know if I should tell him or just keep to myself for a while. I chose the latter.

"What are you talking about?" I was still confused and pretending that I had never seen him ever in my life.

"I was a friend of Jason's," he said putting his hands up to surrender. "He was bringing you to the town where I live."

"Then, why were you on the bridge?" I was still skeptical. "Were you in the other car?" I accused. I was growing frustrated. What the hell was going on?

"No," he said looking directly into my eyes. There was that calm again. The calm that stopped me from crying and my chest pain.

If there wasn't so much else going on inside of my mind, I would have questioned it. Instead, I let him go on. "I was waiting just over the bridge for you guys. I saw the car and then I saw Jason's car go over the bridge. I sprinted toward you. I got you out first and you were breathing so I went over to him next. But by the time I got to him . . ." he trailed off and his eyes looked sad for a moment. "Well, you know the rest."

"Yea." I looked down feeling like I could cry for the rest of my life.

"Come with me," he said abruptly. He nodded his head toward the entrance.

"What?" I stopped in my tracks. "Come where?" Why was I trusting this person? Was I trusting him? I just stopped and looked at him for an explanation. Why am I trusting him? I kept asking myself. I stood there unable to move.

"You don't know me, Lily, but I know you." He took a breath. "My name is Ian and Jason was a boy I have known for a very long time," he said.

There it was, that word, *was*. "Jason has told me a great deal about you and he was the one who set everything up for you. Now that he is gone . . ." He stumbled on the word *gone*. "It is my responsibility to go through with his plan." He put out his hand just as Jason had the first time we met. "Trust me?" Then, something remarkable happened; I took his hand. In some insane way, I did trust him at least at that moment.

"Where are you taking me?" I asked simply without any more bitterness in my voice. I had decided to trust Ian and only because I had trusted Jason. He reminded me of him a little—beautiful and strong. He calmed me. Plus, I did know him. How could Ian have not known that?

"There is a doctor who is waiting to see you." He gripped my hand tightly and we walked together.

"Why is there a doctor waiting to see *me*?" Again, I was puzzled. To me, the last forty-eight hours were a puzzle. The last couple of days had me completely mystified. Why was Jason dead? Where had we been going and why was Ian here?

"Jason had set up this appointment for you. He wanted you to see a doctor for your heart." He said it so matter of factly.

"Jason was an orphan. How could he have possibly set anything up for me?"

Then came the indescribable pain in my head and I was not standing there with Ian anymore. It was Jason! I could see him wearing the same clothes he had been wearing before he died and the blood was still on his face.

"Jason!" I cried out.

"Lily! Come back to me. You would go anywhere with me, right?" I turned my head only seeing the wood of the bridge. He was talking to me like he had not just heard me call his name.

"How?" It was almost like he couldn't hear me. My head! I was still holding it when I was suddenly looking at Ian again in the hospital. I was sitting on the floor and Ian was bent down in front of me. My face was hot and I could feel the tears streaming down my face.

"Ian, what is happening?" I knew that Ian would always tell me the truth.

"Hey," Ian started gently. He looked like he didn't want to touch me but then I remembered the bandages all over me. The bandages that Jason had put on me. I wanted to die all over again! I could almost feel him with me. "Are you ok, Lily?" Why did everyone ask me that?

"No," I said briskly, "I am still not ok."

What the hell was that? Another dream? Another premonition? Was it really happening and this was all just a nightmare? I was alone. That was all I knew at that moment—that I was alone and Jason had left me. Maybe the things I was seeing were actually just dreams. I wanted to just come to that easy conclusion but there was still this nagging feeling in the pit of my stomach. I gave him my hand and let him help me up.

"I don't need anybody's charity." I stopped again pulling my hand away.

"This is not charity." He started to look frustrated. "Don't you ever just trust people?"

"No, I don't." I stood my ground. It was the truth, I never trusted anyone.

"Do you still trust Jason?"

"I always trusted Jason," I shot back at him.

"I'm sorry, baby girl."

"What did you just call me?" A look that could definitely kill! "Do not call me that." This time, I looked him in the eyes. Those green eyes look so familiar and calming. In a vision, he had told me that he would always be there with me. Was this one of those times?

"I'm used to Jason talking about you." He looked almost embarrassed like he screwed up. "Please, Jason set this all up." His voice got calmer and he looked at me like I was a child. I considered for a moment and then started to walk with him again. Jason set this all up? Jason didn't have the money for this, did he? I started questioning everything that I ever knew or believed.

"How?" I asked. I refused to go anywhere until I got some answers.

"Jason's parents died when he was young," Ian began.

"I know that already." Ian was getting frustrated with me. Ian was always so happy and I was actually frustrating him. That gave me some satisfaction in some sick way.

"Jason had no other family. His parents were extremely wealthy. They had left him with a trust fund that he would get when he turned eighteen."

"What?" I whispered to myself.

I took a deep breath in memory of my sweet Jason. I reached out for Ian's hand again and he took mine in his. It felt good to have someone, anyone to hold onto right now. And even though it was all soothing and helpful, I couldn't help the nagging feeling in the back of my mind that I knew this man. Had I been here before? It sounded crazy but I couldn't shake the feeling. I felt like this had all happened before or this wasn't real. I could not figure it out but I was sure that I was going crazy.

Dr. Robert Hope was very friendly and kind. "You must be Lily!" he said cheerily. He took my hand to shake it. He was a middle-aged man with salt and pepper hair. He was even quite handsome for a man in his mid-forties maybe. Then he shook Ian's hand and they smiled at each other.

"I will just sit over here." Ian went to a chair in the waiting room.

"Ok, Lily," Dr. Hope said putting his hand on my shoulder and I flinched. "Let's go get started." I have forgotten about my bruises. He took me back behind a door to where there were a bunch of examining rooms. I hadn't been to many doctor's offices but it looked abandoned. There was no one at the front desk and no nurses or anyone there but the three of us. I thought it was strange but today had been so horrible and strange anyway so I just let it go.

I sat up on an examining table. I felt the paper crinkling beneath me. I looked around the room. There wasn't much there. I noticed two chairs, one for the doctor and one for someone else. There was a counter with a sink and other utensils.

Dr. Hope had left me alone for a while, claiming he to go get a machine. That is exactly what he came back with. It was a machine with attachments to it. My heart started to race and all of a sudden, I didn't feel well. I started to sweat and feel dizzy. The doctor noticed.

"Hey," he said softly, "why don't you lie back?" He said, touching my shoulder. I lay back and took some deep breaths. I was really wishing that Jason was here to calm me. I breathed while he took my pulse and noticed a picture on the ceiling of a white sandy beach. Was that supposed to help people calm down? I almost laughed out loud. I rolled my eyes but I could feel the blood rushing back to my face and the ringing in my ears stopped. I stopped sweating but I felt a little uneasy after that episode.

The doctor set up the machine. At least, that is what it looked like he was doing. Then, he pulled out a gown for me to put on and left me alone to do so. I started taking off my shirt and bra, the shirt that Jason had bought for me not twenty-four hours before that. I felt pain in the pit of my stomach again. It was a sadness of wanting to be with him again. I shook off the feeling for now. *I can fall apart later*, I thought to myself. Then, I changed into my gown.

A couple of minutes later, the doctor knocked and poked his head in.

"You ready?" he asked. He put something cold on the microphone-looking thing and then touched it to my chest. I jumped. Partly because I didn't want to be touched there and partly because the gel was cold.

"I'm sorry, dear. All I'm doing is looking at your heart. See?" He pointed to a screen in black and white and I could see my heart pumping.

"Is that . . .?" I started to ask.

"Yes, that is your heart. I'm going to just take a few pictures to see what I am looking at."

He probed around my heart for a bit and when he was done, he handed me some paper towels. I assumed they were for the gel.

"You can go ahead and get dressed now and I will be back to talk to you." He left the room and I dressed quickly. I sat there for the longest time waiting. What was he doing? The longer I sat there, the more nervous I got. What was he doing? It wasn't like he had any other patients out there and my patience was now wearing thin. I was exhausted from everything that was happening and all I wanted was for Jason to smile at me and hand me a bottle of whiskey. I would take anything right now that would help me to just go to sleep and forget.

I stood up and started to pace. My heart started up again and at that moment, Dr. Hope walked in again.

"Lily, please have a seat." I sat in the chair in the room.

He sat in the other chair and he talked to me about my heart. I knew it was bad, but I guess I didn't know how bad.

"Lily, you shouldn't even be alive," he said softly. "I scheduled you for surgery in a week. I believe that I can begin to make some repairs to your heart."

"Surgery?" I asked. It was more for my benefit than for his.

He paused to look at me. What was he looking at? Was it to see how I would react? I said nothing. I felt nothing. To be honest, at that moment, I did not really care if I lived or died. But I said nothing.

"Medicine has come so far since you were a baby," he went on. "To be perfectly honest, Lily, you should be dead by now."

"So, I have been told," I said quietly.

"I believe I can help you," he said. That was all for a few moments at least. Just when I was about to get up and leave, he spoke again. "I went ahead and scheduled your surgery for a week from now. I still need your permission though, of course."

"I can't afford some fancy surgery," I said standing to my feet.

"Lily." He sighed. "It is already taken care of. So, think about it and I hope to see you in a week."

He handed me a card with his name and number on it. I opened the door and walked out into the waiting room. Crap! I thought to myself. **He was** still here. I looked at him and the amount of concern I saw there was incredible. He was acting as if he knew me. Could Jason have possibly talked about me that much?

"You are still here." I glared and cocked my head to one side. He only looked at me and I felt all of my anger leaving my body. My heart was slowing to a normal rhythm. The only person I knew who ever had that effect on me was Jason and it made me miss him even more. This day just keeps getting weirder.

"I am," he said standing up. "Shall we go?"

"We?" I almost spit out the word. My voice was rising now. I grabbed at my chest. I sucked in a breath. I could hear Jason in my head. "Breathe, baby girl." I felt like I was going to walk out of this room and he would be there waiting for me. All I wanted was for him to be with me right now.

"Hi, I am Ian." He puts out his hand for me to shake it and for some strange reason, I do. I was breathing slowly and I looked up at him. He was at least a foot taller than me. He was handsome, I noticed. Why was I noticing that now? "Lily," I said.

"So, where are we going, Lily?" We were standing in front of two elevator doors. He pushed the button. I didn't say anything and then "ding." "Up or down?" He cracked his cheerful smile, the one I used to love. At the moment, it was really annoying me.

"Why don't you tell me?" I stare ahead. "You are the one following me, remember?"

"Yes, I do remember." Again, he is cheerful. I thought that he and Jason had been friends. So, why was he acting so happy or at least so ok? I wanted to strangle him.

We walked through the lobby toward the exit. I stopped right before we left.

"What is it?" he asked gently.

"Jason," I said. That was all I could get out. I couldn't leave him. Or maybe I didn't want to leave him. Ian touched my arm and I jumped. My head started to feel cloudy. My ears started to ring and I thought I heard Ian say, "It's ok, baby girl, just breathe." What? Did I hear right? Maybe I just wanted Jason here with me. I felt arms around me and then it went dark.

CHAPTER TEN

I woke up on a bed in all of my clothes. I sat up gasping for air and looked around frantic. Where was I? I was in a small room with wooden furniture and a bathroom straight ahead. I looked down at the crimson sheets. Jason? No, he is dead. Dead. My sweet boy was dead and I started to cry. Suddenly, Ian came out of nowhere, I swear.

"Shhh . . ." He was soothing me. "Lily, it's ok." I looked at him and it all came back to me. I was in the hospital getting my heart checked. Ian was there. Ian. I was still mad at him. I started to shake as I remembered everything going black and now, I woke up here. *Here!* In a room that was perfect. A room that only Jason could have put together for me. The tears and the shaking came. Out of nowhere, Ian got up and went into the other room. My hands were shaking. They wouldn't stop and I thought I knew why but I never cared before. I didn't really care now.

Ian appeared again with a shot glass. I looked at him confused and almost embarrassed. Nevertheless, I took the shot glass and it was my whiskey, the same brand that Jason and I drank every day. I hadn't noticed it then, but I did drink a lot more than Jason. I always told myself it was because of the abuse . . . and maybe it was. After taking the shot, my hands started to calm and I wanted more. However, I said nothing. I just looked into those beautiful green eyes, then my heart began to calm down.

"Where am I?" I asked

"You are in Believe, Oregon," he answered seriously. He wasn't smiling, so I didn't feel the need to strangle him at the moment. All I wanted was to know what the hell was going on!

"I don't understand." And I didn't.

"This is where Jason was taking you," he said calmly. "You should try to go back to sleep." He stood up and something was strong inside me. "You have been through so much." No kidding, I thought to myself.

"Where are you going?" He must have heard the desperation in my voice because he came back and sat down on the bed next to me. He hesitantly put his hand on my head and I let him. I laid my head against his chest and fell asleep.

I woke up and the sun was out. This time, the room was filled with light and I could see all the little things that were meant for me. I looked down at the beautiful crimson sheets and grinned. As quickly as it came, it was gone. He was gone.

I got out of bed and the wood floors were cold beneath my feet. As I walked to the bathroom (which was only a foot in front of me), I heard voices coming from the other room, a room I hadn't even seen yet. I had so many questions and people were going to start answering them. For now, I stood and eavesdropped on who I recognized as Ian, but I did not know the second voice. I could tell it was another man and that they were arguing in hushed tones, trying not to wake me, no doubt.

"What are you doing here?" Ian sounded upset.

"I want to see her." He sounded cold toward Ian.

"You are not what she needs right now," Ian said.

"I am exactly what she needs, I am the reason that she is here." He sounded like he was about to get angry.

"She doesn't know you," Ian said more urgently.

"She does not know you either." I could hear the anger in his voice, then suddenly, I recognized his voice but it hadn't been so angry. Where did I know that voice from?

My foot must have made the floor squeak because they stopped talking abruptly and I heard Ian close the door. What were they talking about? Me. But why? I felt like I was right in the middle of the twilight zone. I had no idea where I was, who I was with, and my best friend was dead. I sighed and walked into the bathroom closing the door behind me. I needed answers. At that moment, all I wanted was to get into a hot shower.

I came out of the shower and there were all jeans, t-shirts, and sweatshirts in the drawers and closets. Everything fit perfectly in true Jason style. I quickly threw something on, putting my wet hair in a bun, and walked into the next room. The room was empty. It was a good-sized room and the kitchen was small but had all brand-new appliances and countertops. Then I did something I had to do. I started to look for the whiskey. My body had started to shake in the shower. It had to be here somewhere I thought as I opened every cabinet and the freezer. Then, there was a knock at the door.

"Ian." I faked a smile as I opened the door. "I thought that you were already here."

"Looking for this?" He held up the bottle and I went to reach for it. He was faster and pulled it away. "You shouldn't be drinking," he chastised.

"I'm sorry, since when are you in control of anything in my life? You don't even know me!" I looked at his face and for just one instance, he almost looked angelic. He thought for a second and then handed me the bottle. That was unexpected. I took it anyway and took a swig as quickly as I could. That was better.

"He didn't get to finish it." He sounded sad as he walked past me into the loft.

"He was doing all of this?" I asked. Of course, he was. The bedroom was all me and all the clothes. What a stupid question for me to ask.

"Yes, he was. But that night, he called me frantic. You were unconscious in his arms and he was scared. So, he just drove you straight here."

"You were friends?" I was trying to warm up to Ian but I couldn't. I definitely did not want to get attached. There was no way that I was staying here. Where is here? I thought of it so intensely that I said it out loud.

"Where is here?" I was getting frustrated. I had a mix of emotions that I didn't know how to deal with. As a matter of fact, I never dealt with them . . . I drank them. I took another swig of whiskey then Ian grabbed it away from me.

"Ok, drinky, that's enough for you." He smiled again. "I'll give it back, I promise."

"'Drinky?'" I gave him a dirty look. "Maybe I wouldn't be this way if he hadn't just left me. I should be dead, Ian!" I was so angry that Jason was dead and that I was stuck in a place that was full of Jason with a very nice person I didn't even know. I wish I felt bad for being mean to him but I really didn't.

"Baby girl," he said softly.

"No." I pointed my finger at him. I closed my eyes for a moment to keep myself from screaming.

"Me!" I yelled. "You left me all alone in this world and since you left, I had a miserable and terrifying life alone! Then, I finally found someone who I loved and could depend on and he dies!" I turned away from him and started to cry. I kneeled down on the hardwood floor.

"I am sorry." And he sounded sincerely apologetic. This was Ian, my angel. Of course, he was sincere.

"How did you do this?" I whispered to Jason. Ian must have known that I wasn't talking to him because he didn't say a word. He just stood there looking at me, waiting. It felt like Ian knew every move I was going to make before I made it.

"Let's go," I say wiping my tears with my sleeve. I wore the jeans and black hoody that we bought from Walmart.

"Where do you want to go?" Ian almost sounded confused, which amused me because he was always so confident or at least it seemed so. I went into the room, found my shoes and socks, and put them on quickly. I had no idea where I wanted to go. I had no idea where I was but I did know that I needed Jason. I was going to the bridge.

"I need to get out of here and you have some explaining to do." He actually looked stunned. I cracked a smile and then, so did he. Shit! I was not getting attached. I was determined not to, but he was the only person I had right now. What was I doing? Then, I said the same thing that I always told Jason when he asked me where I wanted to go. "The bridge," I said.

We were on the third floor. I opened the door and walked right into the staircase practically. We took the stairs.

"Really? The third floor?" I looked up again. I was talking to Jason and again, Ian seemed to know and maybe even understand. Ian silently walked behind me. My heart began to hurt when we finally got to the bottom and I was feeling dizzy.

"Lily?" Ian sounded scared.

"I'm ok," I said but my breathing was heavy. He put his hand out and this time, I let him touch me. As soon as he touched me, everything stopped hurting. The amazing calm came over me again.

This is important because this is part of me. It was a courtyard in the middle of three buildings. There were three benches around the circle. They looked old and new all at once. In the middle of this circle was a water fountain, like a real stone fountain, the kind you see in ethnic front yards. But there wasn't a statue made out of stone. Instead, it was all-white stone and the water pooled at the bottom like a normal fountain, but instead of a statue, there were words. Right in the center, the *words* were stacked right on top of each other and each word had a stone. Peace-blue, patience-black (probably because I had none), hope-red like a ruby or just maybe they were actual jewels, and love-a diamond. The water trickled out of the top and flowed down the words. I stood there in shock. How could this be? I walked up to it and felt the water run over my hand. It was incredible! How on earth could *Jason* have had this done? I looked back at Ian and he looked at me curiously.

"What?" I ask.

"What does this mean?" His green eyes soothed me for a moment and I forgot what I was going to say. Then, I shook my head.

"I have no idea." There was the de ja vu. I knew this fountain. But from where?

"It's ok, Lily," he said cautiously.

I looked back at the fountain. There was no mistaking that it was remarkable and completely unique. There was a little ledge. I sat down for a minute feeling paralyzed. *Jason* did this? Something didn't sit right with me. Right in the middle of my thoughts, Ian broke through.

"You wanted to go to the bridge?" he asked curiously. I turned and for the first time, I saw something in him. I saw a kind person with eyes I could see into and hope. I saw hope just like the day I met Jason. He was dressed in jeans and a black t-shirt. He smiled at me again. Ian was always smiling—always!

"You do know that you can be really irritating, right?" I glanced at him.

"So, I have been told," he said thoughtfully.

"Here we are," he said. I looked up. We were standing on the bridge. I stood there in the middle of the bridge and looked out across the lake into the pine trees that never seemed to end. It was almost exactly like the bridge we used to go to outside of Seattle. My chest started to hurt and my head felt dizzy. I woke up in the water but Ian was there, picking me up out of the lake. He was bringing me to the bridge. I didn't see Jason anywhere. I was cold and wet, and Ian was there making sure that I was breathing.

"Lily," he said it over and over. Then I saw *him*, the angel from my nightmares, but he wasn't scary. He was there to save me and this girl with bright red hair. They were all standing around me on the bridge, this bridge.

The vision seemed to just fade away and I was back on the bridge with Ian perfectly normal as when we first got there. Normal?

What the hell was normal anymore? Ian and I were sitting on the bridge and he was holding me.

"Where am I?" I started to panic. Ian must have caught on because all of a sudden, this incredible peace came over me and my heart slowed. I still knew that something wasn't right.

"Hey, shh."

"Who . . ." My heart was racing and my ears were still ringing and I was gone again.

I heard voices but I couldn't move. Jason? No, Jason was dead. Right? So then why could I hear him? Why did my body feel heavy? I tried to speak. I even tried to listen but my concentration was not there. Then, he was gone. Jason was gone again. His voice was gone and I woke up.

"Hey, baby girl," he soothed. He was always soothing. "Where did you go?"

"Down the rabbit hole." It was all I could think to say.

"I'm sorry." He looked uncomfortable.

"Will you help me up?" I asked. His strong arms were around me and I could feel the sweat dripping off of me.

He gave me his hand and I got to my feet. I was still slightly unstable so there he was still holding me up. He was holding onto my arm and it didn't hurt. I had no idea why that thought suddenly came into my head but it did. I looked and my bandages were gone.

"You have a habit of scaring me to death. Where did you go on me? Are you ok?" We were standing so close but not touching. He wasn't comforting me for once. Where did I go?

"I don't know," I say. The bridge was almost quaint, made out of wood and clearly kept up. But this was the bridge that changed everything. "What is happening?" The tears finally came. He walked up to me and I backed away.

"Why don't you tell me what happened?" he suggested.

"It seems like ever since I met Jason, I've been hearing voices, and just now, I was on the bridge and there were three people there. You were one of them. You were pulling me out of the water. This water!" When I said it out loud, I sounded crazy, but what else could I do? Who else could I talk to?

"What is it that you want to know, Lily?" He looked so concerned and frustrated at the same time. What the hell was *his* problem? I was the one confused and alone. My mind was doing one thing and my body was doing another. At that very moment, all I wanted was a drink. Jason is not here. The drink will take away the pain.

"I want a drink." I pushed past him.

"You can't drink before the surgery, Lily." He sounded like he was my parent.

"Shut up!" I yelled. "Ian!" I shot at him.

My heart started up again. I always thought that somehow, Ian could hear it because he came up to me. I turned away from him. He was the nicest person I had ever come across in my life and was pushing him away just like I did with everyone else. Jason would not have wanted this. He would not have let me isolate myself.

My heart started to ache and I felt dizzy again. I always thought that Ian knew when I was about to pass out because he seemed to come get me and soothe my panic or my pain immediately.

"You still with me?" he asked. I guess when you are with someone who passes out on you all the time, you start to worry.

"I am," I said quietly.

CHAPTER ELEVEN

He carried me up three flights of stairs and into the bedroom. We sat there for a while. I cried and leaned against him. Then I looked up at him.

"Ian?"

"Yes, baby girl?"

"Do you know me?" We both just sat there against the headboard. He looked sad.

"Of course, I do, baby girl."

"What is happening to me?" I asked. I wasn't sure I wanted to know much more right then.

"Truth?" he asked and I smiled a little.

"Truth."

"I don't know, Lily. Where did you go on me today?" His voice cracked like he was scared. I never remember him being scared even in the last couple of days.

"I told you. I could hear Jason though. Like really hear him."

"Jason?" he asked. I saw some relief on his face. Was he expecting me to say something else?

"Yes." I lifted my head to look at him. "Ian, I am sad and alone. What is happening to me?"

"You are not alone." He touched my nose with his forefinger like I was a child. He seemed so familiar to me. This whole place felt like de ja vu to me, like it had all happened before.

"But Jason was just like me. He was in the foster system. How could he do all of this?"

"Maybe you need to ask him." He got up and left my beautiful loft.

What the hell did that mean! How could I ask him? He was dead! What the hell did any of this mean? None of this made any sense. Where was I? Why was Ian here? I always thought that he knew things, but maybe he doesn't know at all. Maybe this is all a bad dream. I laid down and cried. I cried because everything hurt! I cried myself to sleep alone that night. I had no more comfort that Jason was just next door in his bed.

The next morning, there was a knock at the door. Was Ian knocking now? I got up and opened the door shaking. At first, I thought no one was there and then I looked down at the cheeriest four-foot-tall girl I had ever seen. Her hair was short and a beautiful red—red like an apple, not like Ruby's dull red hair. She had a bottle in her hand. Why was everyone showing up with alcohol for me?

"Hello!" she said. "My name is Rose and Ian sent me over here today."

"Lily," I said, "but I'm sure you already knew that." I was back to my old friendly self again. She walked in right at me handing me the bottle. I opened it immediately.

"Oh my," she said looking around.

"What?" I squinted at her. I was not awake at all and it was way too early for Rose!

"Oh nothing," she smiled and walked around a bit. "Ian was right! We do need to go shopping!"

"Shopping?" I asked. "For what?"

"Anything you want really, but maybe some furniture."

I snorted, "Who is going to pay for that?" I was beginning to feel like I was in the land of Oz.

"Don't worry," she said, "it's all taken care of."

"Of course, it is." I rolled my eyes.

"Ok, chop-chop. Go get ready." She shooed me into the bathroom. It hadn't occurred to me that I had not even showered in a couple of days. She didn't fight me for the whiskey so I took it with me. I looked at my healed body. I no longer had any cuts or bruises. I wasn't bleeding. I stood under the hot water. Suddenly, I had a pain in my chest. I was showering and I finally looked well. But Jason wasn't here to see it. He only saw the bad stuff. I let my mind wander for a bit. We had never made love. If I knew Jason at all, it was because he didn't want to hurt or confuse me. He was my first love and my first real friend and for what? To be taken away from me?

I didn't care *who* was waiting. Before leaving the room, I hid the bottle of whiskey under my sink. There, I thought, I was set for later.

When I was finally dressed in my usual jeans and t-shirt, I walked out to see Rose. She was stunning like Ian. Her brown eyes were wide and excited. I wanted to kill her! Instead, I pointed toward the door.

"Coffee." It wasn't a question.

"Of course," she said clapping her hands together. "Anything you want." She did not seem to notice how much she was irritating me. The more likely answer was that she didn't care. She was this little ball of energy and it was way too early in the morning to handle her. However, she did make it a point to get me my coffee. The car was an old gray Toyota but clean. Everything about her was neat and clean. She wore a perfect white sundress with black flowers. The white looked too white against her skin but she definitely pulled it off. I liked her better with every sip of coffee I took. She chattered and I stared out the window at all of the green. Then, something did occur to me. Rose liked to talk. Maybe I could use that to my advantage.

"Rose?" I asked trying to sound more upbeat.

"Yes?" She was obviously excited that I had entered the conversation even though I wasn't excited at all. I had my own motives. I could almost feel Jason being proud of me. I smiled to myself a little.

"I was just wondering"—I paused because I wasn't really sure what I was asking—"I heard Ian talking to someone outside of my door the other morning. It sounded like he was talking about me." Again, I paused. I saw her cheerful smile falter for just an instance.

"Um, I don't really know." She smiled again. "Why don't you just ask Ian?"

"I just don't know if he will tell me." I looked at her.

"Ian would tell you anything, Lily." She tried to keep her smile. "Ian will always tell you anything that he can." That sounded cryptic. Any normal person would have let that go, but all I heard was that Ian knew something that he might not be able to tell me. Who are these people? Why was Jason so convinced that I would be so safe here?

"It doesn't feel like that." My anger came back.

"Ian always tells the truth. Jason and Ian were really close, Lily. If you need Ian, he will be there." Did she even know what she was talking about?

Rose and I drove to Portland and all she wanted was to shop for clothes and furniture. All I saw was loss. I saw clothes I would never wear and so, I picked out blues and browns that Jason would love. I want to say that Rose and I became fast friends but our relationship was more of an educational variety.

"This sofa is beautiful!" Rose looked so excited at the furniture store. It looked like an antique that I would never sit on or put anywhere. She took one look at my face. "Ok, we can keep looking." She looked so disappointed. I almost felt bad and then I got over it. I wanted what I think Jason would have wanted. All of those times we talked, we talked about what we wanted to put in our place. I love crimson and he loved the blacks and browns.

"See? Our apartment would look great with your splash of red," he had said smiling at me.

So, there I was in a department store without him. He was not here to pick out these things with me.

I looked at many couches. If I picked out a brown, then it would remind me of the foster home. So, I kept walking. Finally, I picked out a beautiful red suede sofa and a matching comfy recliner that rocks. I like to rock. Yes, it's random but it's true. I went with a black coffee table and everything else was black and brown tastefully put together. It had to be. After all, I had Rose with me.

I was browsing around just thinking about Jason and these hallucinations I was having. Yes, we will go with that. I was having auditory hallucinations as well but those seemed to be better after a car crash. I was lost in all of this when Rose came up behind me.

"Lily," I swear I jumped ten feet in the air.

"Rose! You scared the crap out of me." I let out a sigh. "Are we done now?"

"Yes, but you never picked out a coffee machine." She smiled. Her smile sparkled like a star.

"Oh! Yes, thank you for reminding me!" This time, I genuinely smiled at her. "Let's just get the best and most expensive one they have." I smiled at her. Again, it didn't feel right to smile yet. I was wondering how we were going to get all of this stuff back to the loft when Rose just waved her hand as if she was dismissing the store and we left.

She was amazing and maybe if we had met under different circumstances, I would even like her. But we hadn't.

When we finally arrived back at the loft, everything was there. Everything! Even my clothes were put away. Of course, I arranged everything the way I wanted it but this was nice.

"I had so much fun with you today, Lily!" She smiled a sad smile. Then, for once, I had to bend down to hug someone.

"Thank you, Rose. For all of this," I said.

"This was all you, dear." She looked as if she was going to start crying as she left. What was wrong with everyone? I was the one who was dying inside! Jason was my family!

CHAPTER TWELVE

"Jason!" I woke up holding onto the bottle of whiskey. I sat up and looked around urgently trying to remember where I was. I was back in the big bed with the crimson sheets. It made me smile a little. I got out of bed and went into the living room. I thought I saw something outside and so I went over to the window. The first time I saw him, I thought I was dreaming. He was tall and his skin was like milk against the night sky. His muscles were . . . well, he looked strong, stronger than Jason had ever looked. His blonde hair added a very small tint of color to him. His entire back was accented by a big black tattoo.

I went into my bedroom and threw on some jeans and a sweatshirt. It was a little chilly outside when I opened the door to the courtyard. The outside air hit me with a chill. I walked out there and sat on a bench. The fountain was between us and I was sure that he hadn't even noticed me there. He was looking up at the full moon.

"It is beautiful, isn't it?" Those were the first words that he ever spoke to me. At first, I wasn't even sure that he was talking to me. Then, he turned to look at me. His dark eyes pierced at me and I couldn't help thinking that he looked gorgeous. I could not take my eyes off of him and he would not take his eyes off of me.

"It is." That was all I could out. His face was sweet but his eyes were dark and almost unfeeling. I was curled up on the bench trying to keep warm. He walked over to me and sat down. Fire. I could feel heat radiating from him and it shocked me at first.

"You are awake," he said.

"I just woke up," I replied. I curled toward his heat subconsciously.

"I am Andrew." He introduced himself but made no attempt to shake my hand or anything. I started to feel lightheaded but I said nothing. I just shifted.

"Lily," I said nervously. He made me nervous. No, he made me excited. I felt my heart jump a little at his deep perfect voice.

"Lily, that is a beautiful name." He still seemed cold. It was strange to me that someone who gave off heat as if it were fire could come across so cold.

"Thank you," I said looking down at my hands. I sneaked a peek at his blonde hair and his muscular body. My chest started to hurt and the dizziness worse. Part of me knew I should get up and leave. Another part of me didn't want to leave his side. I had never felt that way about anyone before, not even Jason. I wanted to say something but everything that I was thinking or wanting to do since I had gotten here seemed so ridiculous to me. Even still, I continued to sit there next to him. "What are you doing out here so late?" I inquired.

"I could not sleep," he answered me. He was beautiful yet still. My heart began to race again. I felt a pain in my chest. Just for a moment, I thought I heard a cry from far away. I closed my eyes and then it was gone.

"I should go." I felt disoriented.

"Lily," he started, "are you ok?"

"I don't know." That was the most real statement that I had made in a few days. I stood up and so did he.

"It was very nice to meet you." His black eyes found mine. I felt that sadness again. He continued to look at me like I was the only thing that mattered.

"What?" I asked suddenly feeling self-conscious.

"You are just so beautiful." He smiled and it reached his eyes. He made me feel like I was the only thing in the world worth looking at. He made me feel special, at least at that moment. "I hope to see you again soon."

My heart fluttered and I walked away. Where the hell had he come from? Then unexpectedly, he touched my hand and I recoiled from him. When I looked down at his touch, my hand was red and hurting. My body felt heavy and the pain in my head came. I heard the scream in my head again and suddenly, I wasn't there in the courtyard.

It was dark and I could not open my eyes. I heard screaming in the distance but I couldn't figure out where it was coming from. My eyes fluttered but couldn't open. A girl with red hair, I could see her, but only in my mind. Another scream and I tried to move. Then I felt strong arms lifting my body.

"Andrew!" This time, my mind was on Andrew. I felt guilty suddenly like I was betraying Jason. I was confused. Something had happened last night but I couldn't remember what it was. I remember trying to leave Andrew and then I woke in bed

I woke up in my bed the next morning. My throat felt hoarse like I had been screaming all night. The morning was bright and I heard the front door open.

"Hello?" I called out. I was scared. Something had definitely happened last night. What was it?

"It is just me, baby girl." I sighed. It was Ian and I suddenly felt a little disappointed. Was I hoping that Andrew had stayed with me? He came into the room with a cup of coffee.

"Your coffee maker hasn't been delivered yet." He smiled and handed me the coffee. "You look like you've seen a ghost," he said sitting on the bed beside me. Maybe I *had* seen a ghost. He looked at me concerned.

"I—" I didn't know what to say. Do I trust Ian? I had trusted Jason, hadn't I? Right on cue, my heart started to flutter and I felt sick. I put my head in my hands. I didn't know what was happening to me. Was I dreaming? "Ian?" I raised my head to look at him.

"Yes?"

"Something happened last night," I said cautiously.

"You met Andrew," he said. He reached out and touched my hand. It was cool and soothing and my heart began to beat to Ian's own rhythm, slow and steady.

"How did you know?" I asked very surprisedly.

"He told me." He was looking at me as if he was waiting for me to say something more.

"You know Andrew?" I asked.

"Yes, I do." He said solemnly looking down. There was definitely a story there. "We used to be good friends." He tried to smile but he looked like he couldn't.

"How did he make you feel?" That was such a weird question to ask. I raised an eyebrow at him. He didn't respond. He just sat there, waiting for me to answer. What was I supposed to answer?

"I want to see him again." As the words came out, I felt guilty somehow. Why though? Why did I need to feel guilty about meeting new people here? Why on earth would I feel guilty about liking those people? Did I think that Jason would be mad at me?

"Ok," he said, "but Lily, I don't think that's a good idea." He stood up and went to leave. Then, I felt even guiltier.

"Ian." He turned and his sparkling green eyes looked into mine. A lump caught in my throat and I had nothing to say. So, I got out of bed and went into the bathroom. If I could not talk to Ian or Rose, who was I supposed to talk to? Jason was gone. Andrew was the only other person I had met and I felt most comfortable with him.

I stood under the running water once again thinking about these blackouts that I was having. Who was the red-headed girl? The dreams I was having weren't dreams. I knew they were different and I had that spelled right after Andrew had touched me. "God help me," I whispered in the shower. I closed my eyes and took a breath.

"Help you?" I heard a voice. My heart jolted and I looked outside of the curtain but no one was there.

"Ok, Lily, now you are really losing it." I got out of the shower quickly. After I was dressed, I saw Andrew downstairs. I practically ran to him. He smiled when he saw me coming, the same smile that he had last night when he told me that I was beautiful.

"Hello, beautiful," he said walking toward me. His smile was wide and enticing. He opened his arms and for a reason I cannot explain, I ran right into them. My heart started to race against his muscular chest. Today, he was wearing a gray shirt, but I could still see and feel his strong muscles.

"What is wrong?" he asked softly against my hair. He was at least a foot taller than I was and I looked up at him. Today, he was warm like he had a fever. His touch did not burn me today.

"I don't know," I whispered. I think that was the most honest thing I had said since I got to this crazy town.

"So, you keep saying." He put me down and smiled. Again, he gave me this intense look, like he was trying to see into my soul. I smiled at him. He made me smile and that felt so good. He was still dark and mysterious, and yet, I was only really drawn to him. I wondered why that was.

"Can I ask you a question?" I finally got up my nerve. It wasn't just that. I felt comfortable and safe with him.

"Always," he answered.

"Ian said that you and he used to be good friends. What happened?" I was very uncertain asking him because he wasn't the most approachable person. At the same time, he had just lifted me into his arms.

"A girl." He looked down at me and touched my hair. That was the last thing that I expected him to say. I saw sadness when I looked into those dark eyes.

"A girl?" I started looking at him confused.

"Yes, Lily girl." He lifted his hand as if he was going to touch my cheek but then, he quickly lowered it.

"I'm scared, Andrew. Am I the one who is dead?" It was a plausible question since I seemed to be surrounded by angels.

"No, Lily girl." He smiled a crooked smile. "You are very much alive right now."

"What is happening?" I went to grab his hand but he pulled back.

"I'm sorry, I don't want to hurt you."

"The heat?" This I at least understood. He didn't say anything more.

"Lily, you have no reason to be afraid. What are you afraid of?"

"I keep blacking out and hearing things. Ian won't talk to me about what is happening and I am supposed to have heart surgery in four days. I am confused and terrified and now you are telling me that you all know me?" His dark eyes blackened for a minute and he looked tired.

"What do you think is happening?" he asked. That was a question no one had asked me this whole time.

"I'm not sure." I looked down. "Everything that I am hearing and seeing has been happening for a while. Actually, they started when I met Jason." I was almost thinking out loud to myself instead of speaking to him. I started to get frustrated with myself. I think he could see it because I inadvertently put my hand on my chest.

"Are you in pain?" Again, he was the only one who didn't seem to know everything about me. That was sort of comforting to me. "A little." He backed away and the pain subsided like it normally did.

"No, I'm ok." I looked up into those dark eyes and saw something. Was it emotion? He was usually so cold and calculating, like when I heard him speaking with Ian the other day. He never sounded that way when he was speaking to me or walking with me. Still, after my episode, he seemed to keep his distance from me. I was hoping that he had wanted to comfort me.

"Do you want to just keep walking with me?" he asked. He sounded young and free. I wanted to be close to his warmth and in some ways, I could see that he did want to be close to me. He excited me in a way that no one else ever had. He gave me goosebumps and every so often, he would put his lips to my hair so I could feel his warm breath on my head. When we came to a stop, I looked up and saw it. It was beautiful with an open green space and granite headstones everywhere. I had no idea how I would afford anything for Jason but I knew that was where I wanted him. It was a cemetery. He took my hand and we walked along a road beside all of the headstones. My thoughts immediately turned to Jason. I had not gone to pick up his ashes yet. I looked around and felt a great sadness. I missed my friend.

"This is the place." We stopped walking. "This is where you can bury your friend in peace." I was speechless because I had forgotten about the ashes. I was suddenly wishing that he had not brought me here.

"Lily, he isn't here anymore no matter where you bury him." Normally, I would have a quick comeback and get angry but he was just like Jason in some ways. He had the ability to completely disarm me. In some ways, he was more enhanced than Jason had been because I could not be mean to Andrew at all. Any time I had started with a smart-ass comment, the words would get stuck in my throat. I never wanted to hurt this amazing person.

"Will you bring me to get his ashes?" I asked quietly. Tears started to flow and Andrew pulled me into his arms.

"You need something to do," he said. I looked up confused. "Since you have gotten here, you really haven't done anything and I think you need something to do."

At that moment, I heard another scream. I looked around and then up at Andrew.

"Did you hear that?" I asked urgently.

"Hear what, beautiful?" His eyebrows furrowed as if he was trying to see what I was thinking. "Is there something wrong?" Every time he asked me that, he sounded so concerned and loving.

"You didn't hear that? That scream?" I asked.

"No," he said shaking his head. "Lily, you are turning white." My heart was hurting and I felt my head getting dizzy. I closed my eyes and let myself fall into Andrew's arms. Then, I saw her again. This time, the girl was blonde. This time, she spoke to me.

"It's time," she said. "It's time to go home." I could feel Andrew's arms around me still but I was enticed by this beautiful girl. What had she meant? Who was this beautiful angel?

Her eyes flashed red and the next thing I knew, I woke up in Andrew's arms. Unlike Ian, he did not ask what I saw or where I had gone. Actually, Andrew acted as if nothing had happened at all. He took my hand and we started to walk back. When we made it to the loft, he walked me upstairs. We stood outside my door. He gave me a quick kiss on the forehead and it was hot. There was something so enticing about that heat I could not explain it if I wanted to.

CHAPTER THIRTEEN

"Do you want to come in?" I asked not wanting him to go.

"No, beautiful, I have to go but will I see you later?" he put it into a question.

"Yes." I smiled and watched him walk away. When I went inside, I saw that my new amazing coffee maker had arrived.

"Lily?" I heard a voice coming from my room.

"Yea?" I answered, sounding annoyed. It was Ian. Of course, it was Ian.

"Hi." He flashed that smile at me and I was calmed. Only since last night, I didn't want to be calm. I wanted to be excited like I was when I was around Andrew.

"Hi." I sat down on the couch. It was nice and soft and I loved it!

"How do you like everything?" he asked.

"Well, I picked it all out so . . ." I paused and decided to be a little nicer. "Everything does look good in here though." He laughed. Why did he always laugh at me? I was always hurting people and their feelings but Ian always laughed like he knew something that I didn't know. He did actually.

"I brought coffee." He looked excited. "Do you want to see how your new machine works?" He started toward the kitchen.

"Of course, I do!" I was a little excited myself and this seemed to please him.

"This is a really nice one," he called from the kitchen.

"Yea," I said plainly.

"Rose, huh?" I could hear the smirk in his voice. "She is actually a really great person once you get to know her."

"I'm sure she is." I was not in the mood to pretend that I wanted to get to know any of them. At that moment, I was even a little annoyed that I liked Andrew so much. I sat there in silence while Ian made coffee.

"Will you take me to get Jason's ashes today?" I blurted out. Ian stopped what he was doing and stared at me for a minute stunned.

"Four days." That was all he said.

"What does that mean?" I barked back. "Andrew showed me a beautiful place to bury him and I want to do something for him!" I was starting to sound like a brat but I didn't care.

"Andrew showed you?" Ian's voice was slow and steady. It was a tone I had never heard Ian had ever taken with me before. So, I quickly changed the subject.

"Four days until what?" I asked.

"Your surgery," he replied but I could tell he was still thinking of Andrew.

"What if I don't want to have the surgery?" I asked but this time, I was a little surer of myself. "No one has even asked me." And the same agitation set in.

"Do you want to die?" he asked. It was like I was making the decision to sign a piece of paper and he really wanted to know the answer.

"What if I do?" I couldn't help the sarcasm. I didn't know if I wanted to die or even what it meant to die, but I knew that no one had asked me what I wanted.

"Lily, I can't help you if you don't want to help yourself." He walked over and handed me a cup of coffee. He looked at me sternly. "You have four days to make a choice."

"All I want is to be asked what it is that I want. Why is that so difficult?" I paused. "I don't even know what I want anymore . . ." I trailed off. "Ian, I have been dying my whole life. Why is it now so important?"

"Jason wanted this for you." He stood there looking at me.

"Will you all stop using *Jason* as an excuse! Jason is dead!" I put the coffee down on the new coffee table and started toward the door.

"Lily." But I was out the door before I could hear another word. I ran down the stairs and out the door. I ran past the fountain and onto the road passing all green trees. I kept running and felt my heart racing but I didn't care. I was angry. I was angry that Jason had left me here alone. I was angry that all of these people I didn't know were trying so hard to help, which I realized at the time was ridiculous, but I just kept running until I could see the water. The bridge was coming up and I was running toward it. It was a beautiful day and I wore shorts and a t-shirt with flip-flops on. Then, I heard that girl's voice in my head.

"It's time." Time for what? What was wrong with me? Ever since I met Jason, I was seeing and hearing things that I was pretty sure were not there. Had I been dreaming all of it? Was I dreaming now? I shook my head. It didn't matter what was happening. I did not want to be here right now. When had I stopped being afraid to die? Was I ever afraid to die?

When I got to the bridge, I stopped and bent over in pain. My chest was hurting and I could barely breathe. I stood up to look over the edge of the bridge. I thought that I would see a smooth river but instead, I saw jagged rocks below and the spray of water up against them. Would I die if I jumped? Or would I simply wake up from a bad dream? I stood there for a long time considering it. Finally, I kicked off my flip-flops and stood there considering all of the possibilities. I climbed over the railing and stood there holding on, looking down at the rocks. My hands started to slip and I closed my eyes. Just as I was about to go over, I heard a voice.

"No!" Then I felt strong arms wrap around my waist and lift me up. I was being cradled like a baby and I realized that I was crying.

I felt the fire coming from the arms that held onto me so tightly. I turned into Andrew's shoulder and cried.

"Why!" I cried out.

"Why what?" His lips were in my hair again.

"Why did you save me? I'm ready to die!"

"Lily, girl," he whispered into my hair. "Not this way. I am here and I don't want you to leave me." What did he mean by "not this way?"

I looked up at him with flushed cheeks and my heart had not calmed down. He looked back with his eyes intense. He didn't even know me. Or did he? Only this morning, he had said that they all knew me. What had he meant by that? Was I dreaming?

"Am I dreaming?" I finally asked as the tears kept rolling down my cheeks.

"No, pretty girl, you are not dreaming." He looked sad for me.

"Then, what the hell is going on?" I raised my voice. I wanted to back away from him and then I realized that I was still cradled in his arms.

"I'm sorry. Do you want me to put you down?" he asked smiling down at me. I didn't want him to put me down. I felt so safe in his arms and warm. Nevertheless, I nodded. He set me on my feet. I stood in front of him with my blonde hair draped in front of my face. I felt embarrassed. I felt like an idiot crying like this in front of him. As I looked into his eyes, I could see that I did not look like an idiot to him at all.

"What the *hell* is going on?" I demanded once again. That was as demanding as I dared to get with Andrew, though in some ways I was afraid of him.

"Do you want me to tell you a story?" he asked, cocking his head towards me.

"Yes," I answered wiping the tears from my eyes. He grabbed my chin gently with his hand. For a moment, I thought that he might kiss me, but in the end, he only said this, "There is no shame in crying."

He lightly took my hand and we started walking. What was all the walking with him? Everyone else had cars to drive and they left the town as needed, but not Andrew. He walked everywhere and I had never seen him leave the town. Maybe he had and I just never saw him. But there was this special feeling I had about Andrew that I never had before, not even about Jason. He made my heart race in a good way. When I was with him, my entire body was aware of his presence. I was attracted to him and yet, I could still hear Ian in my head warning me against him.

We did not walk very far, just a couple of miles away from the bridge and into the woods a bit. We finally came to a gravel road and as we kept walking, I saw that I was sort of in a driveway. Up ahead, I saw a house—a gigantic stone fortress that no one could enter, or at least that was how I perceived it. I looked at him holding my hand and he looked amazing in his blue jeans and black t-shirt. He almost looked majestic walking alongside me. He knew exactly where he was going and even though that sounds silly because of course, he knew where he was going. He just had an err about him.

"What is that?" I asked in awe.

"That," he pointed straight ahead, "is my house." We kept walking until we reach the front door. Again, it was a fortress. The doors looked too heavy to move. As it turned out, they were too heavy to move. They had been put there just for show. We moved around to the side and entered through a smaller door. To my immediate left, there was a wrought iron spiral staircase that I was in awe of because I loved beautiful and different staircases. This house had to be eighteen rooms at least. I tried to look at everything but he kept dragging me along. Everything was silver or mirrors with jewels that I had never even seen before. It looked as though I had walked into an ancient castle. Finally, we came to another staircase made of marble that came down on both sides. He must have seen my excitement. It was hard not to play with Andrew because with me, at least, he was playful. Even through the dark tired eyes, I noticed that I made him light up.

"We are going up there." He looked at me expectantly. I looked back with that pure excitement. "Well, go on!" He raised his hand up and smiled. I ran halfway up the staircase and then stopped to look down them. He was still standing at the bottom looking up like he was admiring me. I turned and ran the rest of the way up. I looked down at him from the little balcony. I raised an eyebrow and he took the steps two at a time almost laughing. I think that was the first time that I heard Andrew laugh and it was a beautiful sound.

"I'm coming." I could hear a smile in his voice.

We walked down a long hallway a bit until we came to a perfectly normal room with a leather couch and a TV. There was a small fireplace and another seat made of leather. He sat on the couch and I curled up next to his heat. I looked at his perfectly handsome face. His jaw was sharp but soft. His nose was not too long or short, just fitting his face perfectly. Those dark eyes gleamed with joy today. Although he did not touch me, he let me curl up next to him. The room was a little chilly and my heart skipped a beat but it was a good beat.

"How have I never seen this here?" I asked in amazement.

"It's hidden by all the trees," he said playfully, nudging my shoulder, "or did you not notice?" I glared back at him playfully. I could not seem to bring myself to be annoyed with him. There was something strange about Andrew and I wished I could put my finger on it.

"It is beautiful. What I saw of it anyway." I raised an eyebrow.

"You and that eyebrow." He touched my nose. "That look could make me smile for all of eternity and I don't smile." That made me giggle a little.

"Well, that makes me feel honored." My smile faded.

He leaned and his hot lips touched my forehead. My heart skipped another quick beat. I stared for a minute at his lips. They looked perfect for kissing. They weren't too full but just full enough to imagine a wonderful kiss. I couldn't even believe that I was thinking all of these things yet. Jason had been the only guy I had ever kissed.

With Andrew, my whole body was screaming out to touch him and be near him. I must have sighed out loud.

"What is it, Lily?" he asked, looking concerned again. I shook my head.

"It's Jason. I feel guilty I think."

"What is there to feel guilty about?" I felt his heat radiating stronger from his body now. When I looked up, his eyes were dark and disconnected again. Was he jealous?

"When we kissed, I felt like I was betraying him. I am afraid that it is too soon to be with someone else." However, I wasn't planning on meeting an amazing and majestic man who made me feel things that I had never felt before.

"Lily girl," he started. Why did that sound so natural? It felt like he has known me forever and it just comes out naturally. "The love of my life told me once that the most important thing to do is to be true to yourself."

"You have someone?" I felt myself getting jealous immediately. I must have been radiating heat because he smiled quickly. It was like he was happy that I was jealous and the heat was calming down. But then, his eyes turned a deep black again and there were dark circles forming under his eyes. This was why I was afraid of him.

"No, she is gone." And there it was. That was what the darkness was about. "I spent many, many years waiting for her to come back to me." He tried to smile again but I saw that he couldn't.

"What happened?" I asked. At that exact moment, I felt a connection between Andrew and I, not the way people say that they have a "connection" with someone. I mean I felt that I could actually feel him. I could feel the pain he was in and it *was* dark.

"You showed up." He looked at me still dark. His hands unexpectedly became very cold as if I was getting sick but I didn't feel sick nor cold. I needed to take his hands in mine and this cold countered the heat. That was weird. It was more than weird! I was now convinced this was all a dream. "Lily?"

"Oh, sorry, I was just thinking." However, his heat had calmed down.

"Stop scaring me!" We were still holding hands.

"Ian keeps saying that too." I almost laughed. "Be true to yourself, huh?"

"Are you?" he asked, looking at me expectantly.

"All I know is that you are the one person I feel I can trust since Jason died on me, and I always want to be with you. In that case, then yes I am." This time, he sighed out loud but it was more of a sigh of relief.

"Then, you have nothing to be worried about." We held hands for a while before I remembered that there was a reason I was here in the first place.

"I thought that you wanted to tell me a story?" I inquired further.

"Do you believe in angels?" he asked. All of a sudden, Ian's face ran through my mind, then Andrew and Jason. I wasn't sure how to answer. He put his warm hand in my head. I could tell that he was trying to calm me but instead, he was exciting me. It sent a tingling down my back.

"I don't know," I answered thoughtfully.

"Lily girl," he began, "I have known you for a very long time. We were young together." What he said was so unreal. How did we know each other?

"What do you mean?" I asked. He looked only a few years older than I was, younger than Ian but older than Jason. He hesitated for a moment.

"I want to tell you everything but I can't."

"What?" I sat up on my knees and looked at him. "Why not?"

"Because I made a promise that I wouldn't." He looked extremely uncomfortable.

"A promise?" I looked at him confused. "A promise to who?" He wasn't making any sense.

I kept staring at him and he at me. Was he hoping that I would remember something? I was trying to remember something, anything, but I couldn't. He looked helpless again and I had no idea why.

"Then, tell me a story." I sat back down and waited.

"Ok," he was almost at a whisper. "There are two kingdoms. One of them belongs to the angels in a place that the human brain cannot imagine and the other belongs to the demons." He stopped and looked at me. I squinted at him and he sort of smirked.

"And?" I coaxed.

"And the angel of death lived in that kingdom and he was in love with the most beautiful angel he knew." He shifted to look at me. I started to hurt and I felt him burning. "She was so pure that she volunteered to fall to earth and help a human, but that meant that he would never be able to see her ever again . . ." he trailed off. I didn't push but when I went to touch his arm, it almost burned me. He drew back from me. He looked ashamed. My skin started to cool as if I was suddenly in the winter snow and I touched him again. This time, my cool skin calmed the fire and he looked at me completely astonished.

"So then, what happened?" I was truly interested now, even though I knew he wasn't just telling me a story. I knew that he was trying to communicate something to me.

"Four days," I whispered.

"Four days until your surgery." He nodded. I shook my head and the tears welled up in my eyes. "Lily, you are dying."

"I know that! Don't you think I know that I am dying?" I was starting to get hysterical. I sat up and put my head between my knees. I was starting to sweat and feel faint.

"Stay with me," he whispered and touched my head. I tried to stay there at that moment but I couldn't. I started to drift.

When I came to senses, I was on the bridge. I couldn't see his face. He was on his knees crying and rocking back and forth saying my name. It took me a minute but I saw that he was on the bridge.

"Please." He was pleading with someone. "Please let her come back to me. I don't want to be without her."

I heard the voice of a woman. "You did this and now someone else is pleading for her life. This is your fault." She spat out at him. She was blonde and gorgeous. She was standing there looking down at him. Her eyes were vibrant but her tone was angry.

"What can I do?" he asked.

"You can pray," she said again angrily. "No. You can hope that she comes back to you. Right now, someone else is protecting her and . . ." the voice faded and I was laying in Andrew's arms. He looked at me expectantly. I felt sick to my stomach. I knew who she was.

"Where did you go, beautiful?" he asked for the first time since I had known him.

"I don't know," I lied. I looked at him and for the first time, he looked small and I could see right through him. It was the first time that someone could not see through me but I could see right through him. I curled back up next to him. I felt the fire coming off of him. I had no idea where I had just been but I knew who the blonde woman he was talking to. She was talking to Andrew. But how? And why? Who were they talking about? This was the story that he was telling me. The thought crossed my mind that he was talking about me, but I also could not comprehend that. How could it possibly be about me? I was just a girl who was in love with a boy who died on me. I didn't even know Andrew. How would I?

I put my head on his shoulder to settle my mind. The last few days had been the hardest of my life but I had no one to talk to. I could not make sense of what was happening. I kept blacking out or dreaming and waking up to half-truths. I was supposed to be in a perfectly normal world and I had this grave feeling that the world I was in was not real at all. I felt that the world I was dreaming of was the real world. Maybe neither was real.

I knew in my heart that it was Ian who would answer that question. What was real? Ian was so familiar and I just knew he would help me. Then, why did I not want to move away from Andrew? I was drawn to him. He told me how he had known me but I had a nagging feeling that he wasn't telling me the whole truth. Who was he begging to in my vision? Vision. That was what that was—it was a vision—something I had never seen before.

"Lily girl," he started but interrupted.

"Why do you call me that?" I asked, lifting my head off of his shoulder and asking sweetly. I did not want to be mean to him. To my surprise, he answered me, which really could mean nothing since he could be lying, and maybe he was. Except the essence of the sentence was true.

"I used to sing to you when you were a baby. But you would never calm down until you would hear me say, 'Don't cry, Lily girl.' You don't remember at all, do you?" I shook my head no. He looked so desperate for me to remember him. Why? I asked myself and then I blurted again. I could not help it with Andrew. Sometimes, you just need someone to talk to and Andrew was my sounding board. I did not choose him. It was like he chose me or something chose *us*.

"What is it that you want me to remember?" There was an edge to my voice.

"What do you mean?" he asked quietly avoiding my eyes.

"I mean that it seems like you and Ian are playing a tug of war with me." I searched his eyes for the truth.

"I mean, of course, I don't remember, Andrew. If what you are saying is true, then I was only a baby." I stood up. There he was beneath me sitting on the couch. Then, he asked an open-ended question that I wasn't expecting.

"Does anyone seem familiar here?" He searched my eyes but I stared at him coldly. "Four days," he said.

"Four days," I responded to him. I was getting upset because I knew somehow that for Andrew, four days did not mean surgery. It did mean something though and I wanted to know what because the truth was that I didn't want to leave him here.

Then, once again, something very unexpected happened. I remembered.

I wasn't there anymore. I was somewhere beautiful with gold and jewels and silver. A sparkling crystal lake was in front of me. Andrew was there and we both were sitting on a color green unimaginable to the human eye with our feet in the water. We sat next to each other and yet apart like we were forbidden to be. We looked about the same age. He stared at me and I laughed.

"What?" I was asking, smiling, and feeling truly happy.

"You are exquisite. Your hair golden and your eyes so blue."

"Are you about to sing a poem to me?" I laughed and laughed as he scowled at me. "Andrew, stop pouting." I hadn't blacked out or anything like that. It was a memory playing in my head. As it faded away, I could feel a strong feeling of love. It came over me quickly and I realized that I had been happy once. I had once been in love and not with Jason or just anyone. I had been in love with Andrew, but from where? I realized at that moment that I had four days to make a decision. I had absolutely no idea what or why. I was still missing pieces.

Andrew looked up at me and once again searched my face. It was me this time who had the power to hide. He couldn't see me. He had no idea what I had just seen in my mind. I had the power to hide it from him.

"Will you walk me home?" I asked and forced a smile.

"Of course." He stood up and we walked arm in arm back to my loft. "Are you ok?" he asked with concern.

"I don't want to leave you either," I said picking up on the cue that he didn't want this night to end. So, he was of course trying to make small talk. I do not make small talk.

"Then . . ." He didn't finish his thought.

"Come on." I smiled that beautiful happy smile that I had in my memory now. We entered the loft and he looked around. He was drawn to the window. The glow of the fountain was there because the sheer drapes were still drawn.

"He really loved you," Andrew commented. "Those are your favorite colors." He seemed deep in thought until I called on him.

"Did you know him?"

"No." He answered like he was sad. "I only knew about him and that he was doing all of this for you." He gestured to the room. "But I never saw it coming."

"You never saw *what* coming?"

"His death." He looked down. "You needed him." Then he looked like he was jealous. Of course, he was jealous! If he and I had something or did in some other universe, of course, he was jealous.

"Another universe," I said softly to myself. Ok, now I was going insane, but considering everything I had just been through, everything was starting to make some sense somehow.

"What?" He looked intensely at me.

"I can see that you know." He startled me for a second because I thought that I could only hide my emotions from him, or at least I had pieced that together.

"*See what?*" I started getting defensive.

"I can see that you are confused."

"Andrew, you don't even know me," I started. "Plus, you do not seem to know anything I am thinking, like Ian or Jason."

"Ouch." He made a hurt face. I quickly changed the subject before I actually did let him see right through me. I wasn't going to apologize either. I was the one who was suffering. But when I looked at him long enough, he wasn't suffering either. At least he looked like he was.

"Why were you here?" I paused only a second. "I mean since you don't live here, why were you in the courtyard the other night?"

He turned to look at me. "I was waiting for you."

"How did you know that I would come?" I asked.

"I didn't." He shrugged. We both wore blue jeans and t-shirts. I was feeling things I had never felt before including happiness but I did not feel sexy. He walked around the sofa and came toward me.

"Do you think I could have been happy?" I asked. "In another life I mean?" He put his hands in my hair. I thought for a moment that he was going to kiss me. Instead, he just whispered in my ear.

"Yes, I think that you could have been very happy." He leaned in and kissed me. The kiss was fire. It wasn't fireworks like people describe. It was fire and when he pulled away, I touched my hand to my lips.

"Did I hurt you?" he asked looking upset. Instead, with tears in my eyes, I lifted my arms so he could pick me up. We kissed and kissed. I cried and cried.

"Oh, my Lily girl." He kissed my neck. "It's me." He was frantic the way he said it.

"I know," I whispered back. In reality, I had no idea but I *felt him*. He pulled back putting me down. Then he began to laugh.

"I used to know you and now, what *she* said is true. You would not be able to see me anymore. *She* said I would have to convince you to love me again and that you would be able to lie to me or that you wouldn't remember. *She* said you might never come back at all. But here you are, standing in front of me and I have been waiting so long." None of his words made any sense to me. I tore myself away from his arm.

I sat on the couch and put my hands in my lap. I had no idea what was really happening. Andrew did, so why wouldn't he just tell me? So, I just asked him.

"Andrew, I have no idea what you are talking about. Who is *she*?"

"You still don't remember?" He looked shocked. I shook my head slowly. He came and sat down on the couch next to me. He looked at me as if he wanted to say something but couldn't. What the hell was going on?

"No, I only keep getting glimpses and feelings, and sometimes, I hear voices and until today, I thought that I had only been dreaming or going crazy!" Now, it was my turn to sound frantic. "I remembered today that I loved you once and I had an overwhelming feeling of love and happiness. You and I are connected somehow. Other than that, I have no idea what is going on." Which was true—that is what I saw. I just didn't tell him about the bridge. "Am I going crazy?" Tears were suddenly pouring down my cheeks. I was afraid. But of what?

"Because I feel like all of this, since Jason died, has been one big dream. I'm scared, Andrew." He put his arm around me.

"Am I hurting you?" I understood now why he kept asking me that. The other night, he had burned me and when I am with him, my chest starts hurting. I realized right then that Andrew was hurting me. There was something that was working against him or someone. I knew it was the girl in my head. I knew her. She had been with me once and I even knew her name even though Andrew did not.

When I am with him, I feel like I could drop dead at any moment in a good way. But there was a difference between Andrew's comfort and Ian's calm. Andrew must have known or he would not be trying to comfort me.

"I wish it was me," he whispered against my ear. I assumed he meant that he was the one who could calm me and knew me. I had so many more questions but I was so tired of asking.

I closed my eyes against his shoulder. I didn't want him to leave. Everything was too scary when he was gone. I must have drifted off because I heard a voice. It was Jason pleading with me.

"Please, wake up baby girl, please." He was urgent. I heard a siren. I couldn't move. "Please, be ok." I felt his hand on my head. I jerked my head up.

"Did you hear that?" I asked urgently and began looking around the room. Andrew didn't have to say anything. I knew it was only me who was hearing and seeing things. It was the scariest thing I had ever experienced. And I had experienced a lot of scares in my life.

"Hear what?" He looked around the room as well. Then, there was a knowing look on his face. He knew that something was happening but I suspected that he knew even less than I did. He looked worried. Pulling me into his arms, he took me to bed. I could not let him leave. I wasn't ready for him to leave. He laid me down and kissed my forehead.

"Andrew," I said in a small voice. "Will you stay?"

"Of course." He smiled and laid down on the bed next to me. I reached for him and we interlaced our fingers. His other hand was stroking my hair. Instead of calming me for bed, my body woke up under his touch. I touched his muscular chest with my other hand. I looked up into his eyes hungry. I lifted my head up toward him. Both of his hands went into my hair and he lifted me up so I was in line with his face and he began to kiss me with his hot lips. His heat was enticing and I kept grabbing for him.

"What are you thinking, Lily girl?" he asked, pulling away from me, from my kisses. I pulled him back to me. He excited me in places that I never thought I would feel there again. When Andrew touched me, none of those memories even came back to me.

Before I knew it, both of my hands were grasping his shirt and I slipped my hand under his shirt to feel the warmth and his body.

"Lily girl," he whispered in my ear. Maybe he was trying to help me remember. But I didn't and I desperately wanted to. "Lily," he whispered again, "we should go to sleep." I moaned frustrated but then I let go. I settled onto his chest and sighed.

"I'm not much happier." He smiled that winning smile at me.

"So then, why are we stopping?" I asked half-teasing, giving him a slight smile.

"Because you aren't ready yet. It would be like being with someone that I didn't know." He sighed.

"Who are you to decide what I am and am not ready for?" I asked a little miffed. I pushed myself up onto my elbows. "If *you* aren't ready, then just say so." We stared at each other for just a second and we both started to laugh, not little chuckles but full-blown I-might-pee-my-pants laughter and it felt so good. There was something about Andrew that made me giddy. I could laugh with him and I fit perfectly in his arms. But in the back of my mind, I knew something was wrong. Then, I had a thought. What if all of these people didn't exist? What if I was going crazy?

"I am definitely ready," he said when we were done laughing. He saw the look of concern on my face.

"What is it?" he asked. It seemed like everyone was asking me that this week and I was tired of it. I squeezed the bridge of my nose with my fingers.

"Are you real?" It was a simple question but it was a loaded one. It was a question that Andrew didn't seem to like.

"Why would you ask that?" He was sincere and had also not answered my question. I raised an eyebrow. "Of course, I am real." He put his hand in my hair.

"Really? Then why do you have that look on your face?" I challenged.

"What look?" He really did not understand.

"You look like you are going to throw up." I could not help but smile a little.

"I am just worried, that's all." He squeezed me tight.

"About?"

"About you, Lily." He paused as if deciding to go on. "You are starting to get scared and that is something that worries me because I don't want you to be afraid."

"Then, tell me what is going on. Because I'm dreaming, hearing things that aren't and can't be real, and blacking out. I'm not scared. I'm terrified that I'm losing my mind!"

"I am real." He put his hand on my face. "Do you feel me?" I closed my eyes. I did feel him. I wanted to stay here in his warmth for the rest of my life.

Andrew did not say another word to me that night. He only held me close and reassured me that everything was going to be all right. Just as I was falling asleep, I swear that I heard him whisper, "I do not want to lose you to the greater good." Was it just a dream?

CHAPTER FOURTEEN

The water was up to my chin now. Fear gripped me and I screamed out. I saw the windows of Jason's car but it was underwater now. I held my breath and dunked myself under as the water threatened to take me.

What was this? Where am I? I was about to let the water take over when I felt strong arms pull me out—out of the car and out of the water. I could not see who it was. I was too disoriented. When I looked up, I saw *his* face. There he was, my beautiful blue-eyed boy, kneeling over me.

"I am here, baby girl." He took my face in both of his hands and kissed me. I was on the bridge. *No.* This was only a dream. Jason was dead. *He* died on this bridge. I had watched the entire thing happen. I had this intense fear that I would wake up and he would be gone. So, I grabbed onto his shirt and pulled him close. My wildly beating heart started to slow down and then, he was gone.

I woke up to a scream. As I sat up in bed, I looked around. The red sheets and the hardwood floors were back. I was alone. I walked over to a drawer and pulled out Jason's sweat pants that I had held onto. I put them on quickly and then sat back down on the bed.

Was that a dream? No, it had happened. Hadn't it? My hair was wet and my lungs burned. I touched my hair. How was I lying in bed completely soaked? Then it happened. The screams came again and again until I realized that I was the one who was screaming. It *had* happened! It was happening right now! So why was I here? Was I dreaming? My reality had just become a nightmare. I stood up from the bed and walked out of the loft.

I looked around for Ian or Andrew. Even Rose would have done right then but there was no one. "What the hell?" I whispered out loud to myself. My heart began to race and I could not stop it. I fell to my knees on the concrete. She tried soothing herself but that didn't seem to be working either. Then, a hand startled me.

I looked up into Ian's eyes. Why was it that someone always seemed to be there with me? This time, he wasn't smiling. He simply sat down beside me and let the calm come me her. I breathed and let my heart slow to a normal beat.

"What was that?" I demanded angrily.

"The bridge." He nodded. But not to me, he was nodding to himself.

"That is happening, Ian!" I stood up and my heart began to race again. The hysteria was coming back.

"No, Lily, it isn't," he said calmly. "It did happen." He tried to touch me but I pulled away from his grasp.

"Jason." I looked at him. "You can't lie to me, Ian."

"You are pulling that card?" He cocked his head.

"He isn't dead," I stated. Then, I got to my feet and started to run. I was running to the bridge.

"Lily!" Of course, he was following me! I got there and looked around. I heard the water. The bridge was empty.

"Yes, it is!" I can feel it in my bones. "You are a dream or a nightmare or something!" I was yelling and could not stop. Ian stood up with me. "Take me there. Now!" I almost felt bad for sounding so mean except what seemed to be happening was too terrifying for me to deal with. I didn't have the patience to care about other people's feelings right now

He did what I asked. We went to the bridge. It was dark and empty and I could hear the water crashing against the rocks. I looked around for several seconds trying to find my bearings.

"Where is he?" I looked at Ian

"Where is who?" He looked so helpless.

"Jason. He was here and he pulled me out of the water." I started to pace nervously. "Ian. My hair is wet! Why is my hair *wet* as if I had just been in that water?" I asked, pointing down to the lake.

"Breathe, baby girl," he pleaded. I couldn't breathe. I could only sit down and cry feeling completely alone and terrified. Then, his voice came from behind me. He was angry.

"You were not supposed to let this happen!" Andrew yelled. He was not talking to me, that I knew.

"I did not *let* anything happen. You know better than that, Andrew." Ian was calm as he always was.

"Do not talk to me like we are still friends. It was *your* job to take care of her all of these years." He must have sensed me looking at him because he stopped talking. It was Andrew, I thought to myself. Andrew was safe and he would help me. My eyes said everything and he bent down to pick me up. I willingly let him hold me. Holding me there seemed completely effortless to him.

"What are you doing?" Ian asked cautiously.

"I am helping her because you obviously can't!" He spat at Ian. "Look at her!" Andrew sounded as if he was about to get hysterical. I warmed in his heat and then recoiled reluctantly from him. He noticed immediately. "Am I hurting you?" Tears filled his eyes. He took a breath and I curled into him again. He carried me all the way to the house. The silence between them was almost comforting. My heart was skipping beats but all I could focus on was Andrew. Even Ian could not pull me away. Ian knew that about us, but I was sure that he thought after they had spoken about all of these things, that I would choose differently. I looked away from Ian. I had to go with Andrew.

"You came," I looked up at him.

"Of course." The cold in his eyes was back. I hated when he was like that. "This is all of my fault, Lily girl. I am so sorry that you are going through this. I definitely did not see this coming." He said the last part under his breath.

"It happened," I whispered against his chest.

"It did," he soothed.

"I loved you too though once," I said, "that was real." Or was still real. I was too confused to decide.

"You did." He sighed softly. "I was hoping that you still do."

"What did you do?" I was curious. I needed to how this could be. How could I have had two lives that now seemed to be colliding?

CHAPTER FIFTEEN

"I am here, baby girl." He took my face in both of his hands and kissed me. I was on the bridge. *No.* This was only a dream, Jason was dead. *He* died on this bridge. I had watched the entire thing happen. I had this intense fear that I would wake up and he would be gone. So, I grabbed onto his shirt and pulled him close. My wildly beating heart slowed and the calm came over me. Then, he was gone.

I woke up to a scream. As I sat up in the bed, I realized that it was I who was screaming. The red sheets and the hardwood floors were back. I was alone. I walked over to a drawer and pulled out Jason's sweat pants that I had held onto. I put them on quickly and then sat back down on the bed.

Ian walked into the loft the next morning. I could hear him come in but I was still tired. Why was I still so tired? I had not been drinking. I felt Andrew move and that's when I decided to pretend to be asleep still. He and Andrew were friends once, good friends. Now, they could barely speak.

Andrew was promised that Lily would return to him and now she had. Soon after, he was told that she would have no memory of him and he would have to convince her to stay with him. Andrew would have to try and help her remember. This has not been easy on his old friend, but they weren't friends anymore. They were on different sides now and Ian was struggling with what to do. Right as Ian was about to go into the bedroom, Andrew came out.

"What are you doing here, Ian?" Andrew was angry. I could hear it in his voice.

"What are you doing here?" Ian countered.

"So, you are answering my question with the same exact question? How original of you." How could he be so mean to Ian?

"You can't have her, Andrew," Ian said softly. "She will go back. This Lily is who we are talking about! You know her better than anyone and she is one of the purest, loving beings that I know. She will do the right thing!"

Andrew looked angrily at Ian. He could not contain his temper this time.

"*You did this!*" He was in Ian's face now. Heat was radiating from his entire body, no his entire being. "You put *him* in our way. Now, my beautiful girl is afraid, no, terrified, and you are not helping her like you are supposed to be."

"She wants you." Ian's anger seemed to fade. Andrew could not stand to be there any longer. "None of this would even be happening to her if it wasn't for you! Why do you think that she is here?"

"You think that you know what this is like, Ian, but you don't. You can't love!" He spat out and I heard the door slam.

Ian looked after his friend and knew on some level that he was right. Ian had never been capable of the love that Lily and Andrew had once shared. He shook it off and went into the bedroom to check on Lily. *He* was her angel and he could only do so much. Feeling completely helpless, he sat down in the rocking chair next to her bed.

When I woke up, I was alone. I sat up looking right at Ian. "Really?" I rolled my eyes.

"Oh, Lily!" he chastised. Ian was always loving. Something was wrong.

"Where is Andrew?" I asked. I must have looked hurt because I got an apology right away.

"I am sorry for the tone, baby girl." He looked tired. Where was my cheerful guardian angel?

"What's wrong?"

"I am tired, Lily." He looked tired.

"Andrew?" He looked up at me surprised. I was not asking for Andrew. I was asking what he had done. Ian seemed to pick up on that quicker than I had expected.

"Lily," he started slowly, "you know." Then it was my turn to look surprised.

"You didn't know?" I smiled at him slyly.

"There is my girl!" He stood up and we embraced. "I mean, this isn't supposed to happen but I have missed you so much."

"Don't get too excited. I still have no idea what is going on. I had memories of us and Andrew. I have no clue what I'm doing here or why."

"I am confused too." He walked into the living room.

"Why am I having all of these scary and crazy premonitions? I'm having memories too and Tempy is in my head, Ian!" I finally had something to say.

"Tempy?" I had forgotten that Ian did not know who that was. I was in the middle of thinking that this was all a huge dream, so could you blame me?

"The princess," I started, "I think that we should all be afraid of, Ian." I felt it deep inside.

Ian turned whiter than he already was.

"She is *here,* Ian! I can feel her." I got out of bed and walked into the living room. I started the coffee while Ian sat on the sofa staring at me. "Stop!" I laughed. Wait a minute, I laughed!

"Lily, I missed you so much."

"I thought that you were always with me." I sat sarcastically. I was still human. What can I say? I was still that girl no matter who or what I had been in the past. He didn't respond. He just looked happy. "What is happening, Ian? Why is she here? Where is here?" I kept pushing.

"I am not supposed to answer any of that. Lily, this is your decision to make. You have to remember on your own and you seem to be." He looked so relieved.

"You mean I have to figure all of this out by myself?" I was scared again. "Ian, I am just a girl who lost the love of her life." He raised both of his eyebrows at me. "Ok, I lost two of them but two separate lives." I was beginning to transcend anything that Ian could understand. Even as the higher being that he was, I knew I was higher.

"You are Lily." He took my hand. "There is nothing to be afraid of, baby girl." I think he was trying to really comfort me. "I have no idea what this must feel like for you. I am so sorry."

I came into the living room and sat down beside him with two cups of coffee. We sat there side by side for what seemed like a very long time. Then, I looked at him.

"Tempy is here." My face was serious and for the first time in a long time, I felt no pain, only a deep hurt.

"Who?" Ian looked at me quizzically.

"Nikki." I could feel my body tensing at that stupid name she had given herself. "The dark kingdom," I started to explain. "The princess." I could see in his eyes that he was catching on to what I was saying.

"You mean that demon Andrew made this deal with?" He furrowed his eyebrows as he struggled to understand. I stopped short and looked at him.

"What deal?" I squinted my eyes at him. Ian had one job and that was to protect me. I also knew somewhere inside of me that he could not lie to me. He averted his eyes. "What. Deal?" I enunciated.

"Lily . . ." I could see that he was trying not to answer my question.

"He could not stand the thought of losing you forever." Ian shook his head.

"He wasn't though." I sat back down. I felt tired.

"He didn't know that."

"So, he went to Tempy." I closed my eyes as I corrected myself. "Nikki."

"Yes." The air was feeling thin. "He made a deal with her to get you back."

"No!" I yelled. I knew her and I knew what the deal was. How could he do that? How could he betray me like that when I had told him about her a million times. I sat down next to Ian and hung my head. "You know that whatever he did was very wrong, Ian." I was about to be hysterical when Ian touched my shoulder and I felt his calm.

"I know, but he still doesn't know that, baby girl." He was trying to soothe me. All I could think of was that Andrew had been tricked. He had let himself be tricked by temptation, quite literally.

She hadn't noticed that she was still shaking and wet when they arrived back at the fortress. She loved to call it that but really, this was built for her too. Andrew had fifteen years to design every intricate detail to her liking. He carried up the staircase and into the small cozy room they had been in before. The fire was burning and he laid her down on the comfortable couch.

"Fireplaces?" I raised my eyebrow

"Good, you seem a little better." He looked at me apologetically. "And you like the heat. You used to anyway." He looked like he was not quite sure what to say next.

"I still do." I smiled back. I really did hate to see him uncomfortable.

He sat down beside her and she curled up next to him. He loved that. It made him feel like he might still have a chance with her. His Lily girl. She was once vibrant and happy.

"Andrew?" I was trying to get his attention.

"I'm sorry, I am just so caught up in you."

"Is that good or bad?"

"I just . . ." he hesitated. "You used to be the happiest girl I knew. You made everyone love you. And now . . ." he trailed off again.

"Now I am cold and bitter?" I looked at him lovingly though.

"Yes," he answered

"Life has made me sad." I looked at the fire in front of her. I was being consumed by flames—Andrew's flames.

"I did something, right?" I knew that something was wrong. I could feel it. Why could I not remember? Why was it feeling like I was in a nightmare that I could not wake up from?

"Andrew, what is happening to me?" I scooted closer to him and looked into his eyes. "I know in my bones that this is real and yet I know still that what I saw had happened."

"I know you do." He nodded. His eyes were cold and yet so knowing. "This is all up to you, my beautiful girl. You have three days to make a choice and I cannot even tell what the choice is. Only you can figure it out."

"And if I don't?" I felt scared again. "Figure it out I mean."

"I hope you do, Lily girl." Now he had looked scared.

He smiled that smile that never reached his eyes. I wondered if he had always been like that. He cupped my face in his large hands and kissed me. We kissed with love and passion that I could not let go of. There was heat this time but no fire. I put my hands on his large muscular arms and could feel his beauty. I felt so small compared to him. My chest was not in pain for the first time that I had been with him. When he pulled away, I wrapped my arms around my neck and held on. Scooping into his arms, he took me into his bed.

He needed me. What if he did never see me again? What if I could not remember? He needed to be with me one last time. I needed him too. I needed his soft kisses and the fire I felt inside. I needed to be there with him, feeling safe. And more than that, I wanted him.

That night, we stayed up talking about everything we could think of. The only thing we did not talk about was the one thing we couldn't. I lay back on the pillows and closed my eyes. My heart began skipping beats again and I felt the dizziness coming on. I turned over to grab Andrew but it was too late. I was gone.

This time, it was more of a dream that I was watching happen. I was in what looked like a palace. It was amazing! The floors were made of gold and there were crimson carpets. There were mirrors every few feet up on the wall. They only reflected the crystal lakes outside and each one had a jewel on them. The rubies were my favorite. I was watching myself walk down the hall and felt every emotion at the same time.

I seemed to be walking a long time and everyone who passed me smiled at me so lovingly. I was happy—no—elated! There was no word for the feelings I was experiencing. I was a higher being; I could feel it. It was so foreign to me but I could still feel it.

"Princess," I heard a boy's voice. I smiled and looked up.

"Abel." I curtsied in my sparkling blue dress. "How do I look?"

"Beautiful." He came down and kissed me on the cheek. He smiled at me so big. I knew him. He was my brother. He looked a lot like me. He walked with me until we arrived in front of two large glass doors.

"Are you coming?" I nodded to Abel toward the doors. He laughed and left me standing there alone. It was a throne room with three thrones. They were golden, jewel-clad, and equal in size. I saw myself walk up to them. A beautiful man walked up to me. I could feel his essence.

"Father." I walked up closer to him. He kissed the top of my head.

"Lily." He smiled and hugged me. "I need a favor of you."

"Anything." I smiled.

"Do not be so quick to answer." He chuckled. Then he told me a story of a child who needed help and it was more than anyone could handle. I heard every word of the story and I felt compelled to say yes. *My* entire essence was so pure and loving. I could not believe that was me!

I walked out of the throne room and ran into Ian.

"Lily." Ian bowed his head.

"Oh, stop it!" I laughed.

"You look amazing!" Ian was beaming at me.

"Ok, we have a problem." I grabbed Ian's arm and whisked him away to tell him everything. After I left Ian, I seemed to be walking around the palace. I climbed a majestic glass staircase. There were two sides going up and a balcony at the top. I stood there looking down over the entire palace. I seemed to really have loved the view of the palace from there. It was my favorite staircase.

I looked down over everything only thinking of Andrew. This was a test. I had told that to Ian. Yes, this was an important task that father could have asked so many other angels to do, but he didn't ask me. He wanted to see if I would pick the greater good over Andrew. Andrew and I had grown up to love each other so much that we had been inseparable for an infinite amount of time now. I knew that was why and so I had to say yes.

I saw and felt everything. It was so strange to feel the feelings of love and happiness while watching it happen like it was a movie. I remembered though that Andrew and I had grown up together. I never remembered a time without him and so we grew to love each other and then to fall in love. We were angels but we still felt, probably stronger than humans did. So, I did not only love Andrew. Our souls were literally connected to each other. I could feel everything that he was feeling and he could feel me.

It didn't matter. The greater good is why we exist. Without us, humans would be completely lost. I had to go tell him, but first, I just wanted to spend some time with him. I started down the staircase and ran right into Andrew.

"Hey," I said, "I was just coming to look for you. Why are you here?"

"I came for you," he said and I smiled up at him.

"How did you know I'd be here?" I asked.

"I didn't." He shrugged and we both laughed. There was no way I could leave him. Those dark eyes only lit up for me. He was a receiving angel. He helped people who were dying and that took a toll on him sometimes. I was the only happiness he knew. What would he do without me?

Ian was there and so was Andrew. It was an interesting sight to see them together getting along. They were talking and laughing. I felt sadness as I walked up to them. There was a connection between me and Andrew that was so strong. I felt the feelings very intensely, but I was watching the scene.

I watched myself watching them. Then, I walked up behind Ian. Andrew smiled at me. It was some kind of a trick.

"Hi, Lily." He smiled without turning around. Ian was a guardian angel but he also had a gift of knowing what is happening and how people are feeling. His intuition worked on them even though sometimes, he could be so annoying. I knew that Ian knew what was happening and so he turned around and put his arm around me. Andrew could not contain his jealousy and then I saw the light go out of his eyes. It was the same as his eyes always looked now.

Looking back at the scene, I saw Ian look at me with a knowing look and put his arm down. "I think Rose was looking for me earlier," Ian said and walked away. I looked at Andrew and walked over to him taking his hand in mine ever so gently. It looked so natural.

"What is it?" Andrew looked down at me. I could feel the love we shared.

"There is something I was asked to do," I started slowly.

"No." He looked as if he already knew and I hadn't remembered telling him anything. I felt confused. I kept watching the scene that was unfolding in front of me.

"No what?" I asked confused.

"You are leaving." He let go of Lily's hand and looked at her coldly.

"How do you know what I am about to tell you?" My voice sounded concerned and even a little afraid.

"I just do." He shrugged.

"You are lying to me," I accused.

That was it. I was back in bed with Andrew again in the fortress. My eyes fluttered opened and the first thing I saw was Andrew's dark eyes again. They startled me because I did not like how his eyes went dark in that scene. Was it a dream? No, I had finally decided that these were memories. It certainly felt like a memory. I sat up and looked at him.

"Andrew." I sounded ten years older if not just wisdom beyond human understanding. It was like with Ian. All of the memories just came rushing back.

"Lily." He picked up on the tone. He looked elated! "Princess."

In my dream, I could tell that Ian was a guardian angel and that Andrew comforted and watched over the dying. However, I sensed that I was something different. I was part royalty. He just reminded me.

"Where did you go?" he asked looking up at me again.

"I had a kind of a dream." I took his hands in mine.

"I did something and you didn't like it." I searched his dark eyes. He said nothing. He couldn't say anything. "I left you." Tears began to run down my cheeks. I had no idea why I felt so sad just like I had been in my memories.

"Shh. Please don't cry, honey. You did something amazing. Your heart is pure . . ." he trailed off.

"The gravel road." I was angry now. He was the one person I wanted to be with right then and I couldn't. I loved him too much to let him see how angry I was. I got to my feet and began dressing quickly. Then, I left Andrew, again. That thought made me sad but I had to keep walking.

"Lily girl." He came after me. "Please . . ." He pleaded with me the way he had pleaded with Nikki. I could not believe he made a deal with her! It was infuriating.

"Do not follow me, Andrew." I spun on him. "This is my humanity being here with you."

"No, Lily." He shook his head. "You love me! You and I were born together and shared everything since we could both remember. You loved me then and you love me now."

"Where are you going?" he asked. I didn't answer him. I got outside and started running. I didn't know what was happening. The only thing I knew for sure was that I was running. I was running toward the bridge. I didn't know what I had hoped to find there but I knew it was a symbol for me. It could be my happiest dream or my worst nightmare. I was the one who was making the decision. I stood on the bridge and closed my eyes until I wasn't there anymore.

CHAPTER SIXTEEN

I opened my eyes and he was there. My poor boy was sleeping. I was in a bed and I couldn't move or speak. What was happening? He woke up and looked at me.

"Lily!" My blue-eyed boy was crying. He needed me, but why? Did he love me the way I love him? "Lily, fight for me!" He bent down and kissed my lips ever so gently. Wow, I had missed him. I closed my eyes and I was back on the bridge.

"This damn bridge!" I could not contain my anger at all. I never could except when I was home. I screamed at the top of my lungs.

"Well, look who is finally here." It was her voice. I turned around looking into her red eyes and Ian was right. I was not afraid of her. She had no power over me.

"Tempy." I was the one who was calm and cold now.

"Really, princess?" The words seemed to make her sick. "You are going to look down at me? Look at where you are and who you are. You are the one who should be afraid."

"Tempy, I will never be afraid of you." I took a deep breath. "You tricked him with your lies and half-truths."

"It isn't my fault that your boyfriend is impatient." She smiled. "I'm here for you, Lily."

"What was the deal?" My disgust showed through.

"Which deal? The one that Andrew thinks he made or the one that he actually made?" Her smug look made me want to smack her.

"All of it." I walked toward her gritting my teeth. I looked at her red hair and scarred face. How could Andrew ever be convinced by her?

"It is not my deal. The deal is for my father." She held my gaze. "Andrew thinks you two are going to go home and live happily ever after." She smiled that twisted smile.

"But really, you want to keep me trapped down here." I already knew.

"He wants you to fail." She shrugged like it was nothing, like this whole situation wasn't hurting the one thing in all the time that I truly loved.

"I will do what I am supposed to do." I glared at her arrogant little face—her true face that showed the evil that was her. She could never show that face to Andrew. I smiled at her and held my head waiting for her to leave.

"Two days, Lily, now that you know the truth." Then, she disappeared.

"Ian." I knew everything now. Most importantly, I knew that Ian was just a call away. And it was so, he came walking up the bridge.

"Lily," he smiled, "I was just worried about you."

"Ian, you worry too much."

"I am a guardian, Lily. It's what I do." He laughed. His smile did reach his eyes and I needed him right now.

"Andrew." I kept focusing on Ian. It didn't matter that I knew what I knew now. I was still human and I still had a choice to make. "My heart is breaking."

"I know." Ian looked at me with great sorrow, probably the same look he had when he lost Andrew.

"It is all a lie."

"I know that too. So, what are you going to do?" He actually seemed like he didn't know. I was a little insulted.

"They need me. Jason needs me and so does Ruby. You really don't know what choice I am going to make?"

"I am sorry, Lily," he was genuinely apologizing. Ian was always genuine. "It's just that Andrew is your soulmate. I can feel the pain you already feel even in your human form." Again, I saw the sadness in his eyes.

"Andrew was supposed to trust me if I am recalling correctly." I put my hands on my hip. Then I was a little unsure. "I am recalling correctly, right?" Ian started laughing and it was contagious. I started feeling dizzy.

"Lily, you ok?" Ian came rushing to my side. "I don't know." Ian nodded at me.

"You are making your decision, baby girl." He held my hand.

"But I still have two days!" My heart started to race. I couldn't leave Andrew again without saying goodbye. "I need to hold on."

"You still have time," Ian soothed. He knew exactly why I was upset and what I was thinking. Again, that could be so annoying. At least, I understood why Andrew always showed up in time. He could feel me.

I looked and there he was, my beautiful angel. Tears welled up in both of my eyes as we looked at each other. I had no words. All I knew is that I was looking at *my* Andrew and I had missed him. How could I leave him again?

"You came," I said. Ian helped me up and then seemed to take a hint. He left us standing there on the bridge.

"I will always come." His voice was void of emotion. The way he looked at me said that he was hurting. He came walking toward me as I grabbed my chest again. He took me into his arms and all I could do was cry. I cried for all the time we had missed and all the time I knew that we were going to miss. "My beautiful, Lily girl," he whispered into my hair, "please don't cry."

"I hate this." I wept into his chest. I certainly did not feel beautiful. The tears would not stop.

"I know," he soothed and all of the coldness melted away from his voice. "You don't have to leave me."

"Andrew." I pulled away and looked up into his eyes. "Why did you do this?" The tears came again.

"Do what?" He looked so innocent and confused. That was the Andrew that I knew. The boy who loved me. How could I tell him?

"Andrew, why would you make a deal with Nikki? Don't you know who she is?"

"I thought I did."

"Then why would you do this?" I was starting to get upset again.

"Because you were leaving me! There was no way that I could live without you. I thought that you had not felt that and then you left." He looked so hurt.

"I wasn't choosing to leave you! I love you! You are my soulmate."

"Then why did you leave me?"

"Why would you take away my free will? Why would you mess with that, Andrew? I never expected this of you." I turned away from him crying again.

"You left without saying goodbye!" His voice was breaking now.

"I had to leave and when I tried to say goodbye and explain everything, you left!" It was all too late now. It was sort of silly to be fighting about it now. But maybe, we needed to talk about this after fifteen years. I pushed myself up onto the wooden railing and sat there looking at him. He came to stand in front of me.

"There is something that you want to tell me," he said taking a deep breath. That was how we worked. We could always feel each other—when something was wrong, when there was something on our minds, or when we were happy or hurting. That connection was something so special and to be cherished. I was the one who could hide from him. Andrew could never keep anything from me but he was the one being that I could hide from. I didn't use that power much just when I really needed to.

"Yes." I looked down for a moment trying to figure out how to tell him this.

"Ok, Lily girl, I can feel those wheels turning," he smirked. "Give it to me straight like you always do." Did I do that? My humanity was still in the way of my complete memory.

"Well, first," I started, "you were supposed to listen to what I had to say all those years ago. I was supposed to come back. I was always coming back. There is a girl who needs my help and that was why I went." He came closer to me and with each hand on each of my legs. My body woke up again under his touch.

"But he could have sent anyone . . ." he trailed off for a moment. I stared up at him waiting for him to get me. "It was a test." He nodded. Then, the little hope that he always had when he was with me disappeared. I felt it leave his body and I just wanted to hold him.

"Yes," I answered quietly. "Andrew, I was always coming back."

"There is more." There was the cold but I could feel the heat rising from him.

"Why would you make a deal with a demon?" It was a rhetorical question and so I went on, "And with one of the most dangerous ones. Do you remember me talking to you about Temptation?"

"Yea," he answered, "you would call her Tempy. She was the princess of the dark kingdom." I said nothing and waited for him to catch on. "That is who she is?"

"That is her."

"But you always described her with black hair and red eyes and the scar on her face." He shook his head in disbelief.

"Yes, and I also told you that she would change forms to deceive."

"So, she appeared to be *almost* as beautiful as you." I smiled a little when he said that. "She knew that she had a better chance of getting me to make the deal." I nodded.

"She changed her name because she knew that you were the only one who knew her name and true form because I had told you. Did you ever think about why she made it so hard for you to be near me?"

"No, because I had no idea about your illness. I didn't think about you in human form." Then it occurred to me.

"You had no idea that I was going to come here." He was innocent sometimes but how could he have known? All I had promised was that I would come back to him. There I was in human form stuck in my veil.

We stay like that in silence for what seemed like a very long time. But every second, I wanted to jump into his arms and wrap my legs around him. The heat felt good on my legs. Finally, he lifted me off of the railing and I did wrap my legs around him. I hung onto his neck and he started carrying me back toward the gravel road. We could both feel the tension between us. There was nothing left to say. We only wanted to distract ourselves.

"My Lily girl," he whispered into my hair as he carried me back toward the fortress.

"Andrew," I whispered back and closed my eyes. I wanted to take everything in—the way he sounded, felt, and smelled. I even wanted to take in this heat.

Andrew's heat was not new but the fire was and the way he could make me sick. She must have done that. But if they wanted me to stay stuck here with Andrew, then why did they make it so hard for him to get to me? That was the one thing that I couldn't figure out.

I pushed that out of my head and came back to my Andrew. By the time we entered the fortress, we were kissing each other long and hard. He stopped kissing me and put me down. I pouted at him and then he pointed at it.

"We are going up there," he said quietly. "I thought you might want to walk." His little smirk came back as he saw my excitement. He was pointing at the wrought iron spiral staircase. I didn't walk up to it. I ran and he ran after me, both of us laughing. I felt free with him. I got to the top of the stairs and he scooped me up again. There was no hallway or door. It was just a beautiful room that was open in front of us. The carpet was crimson and there was one mirror against the black headboard with a small ruby placed at the top. It was beautiful! He carried me to the bed and laid me down on it. It was the softest thing I had felt in a while. He did not lie down with me. He hovered over me holding himself up with his strong arms one on each side of mine. My hands reached up to feel the muscles in his arms. He looked into my eyes and bent down to kiss me softly.

I let him hover over me for a bit while every part of me went crazy before grabbing him by the shirt and pulling him down on top of me. The heat was consuming but my body turned cold and rejected it. I would have questioned that but I was too wrapped up in him to think about it right then. I wanted to stay wrapped up in him.

After we had both gotten so tired of making love, we laid there for a long time in silence while he held me tight in his strong arms.

"Does it feel different for you?" I asked.

"Does what feel different for me?" I could hear the smile in his voice. He was going to make me say it out loud.

"Making love to me." I smacked his shoulder with the back of my hand. We had never done that before here.

"I don't know, Lily girl." He turned me over and looked into my eyes. "I don't have anything to compare it to."

"Now you have jokes?" I laughed. I lifted my head and kissed him lightly on the lips. He put his fingertips to his lips just like I had the first time we kissed and he burned me. "What? I smiled.

"I'm just trying to remember this feeling." He looked sad again. "Please stay, Lily." Tears welled up in his eyes.

"I can't do that," I said almost in a whisper.

"What is going to happen?"

"I don't know."

"Tell me," he said looking deep into my eyes and brushing my hair back.

"Tell you what?" What was it that he wanted to know?

"Why you left." I closed my eyes and remembered that day in the throne room with my father. He had told me a baby who was going to be abandoned by her mother and she needed a strong spirit to help her live. He talked of how this girl would grow up alone and hurting but that one day, she would be needed, and when that day came, she would need to make a decision between her own life or someone else's, and when that decision was made, I would get to come back home and be with Andrew and all of my family again.

"I left because Lily needed someone who was pure of heart." I opened my eyes and looked at him again. "I don't know why I have to go back. I only know that the right decision is to go back because someone needs me to."

"We won't be together now." He closed his eyes and put his head back. "It is all my fault. Why couldn't I be more like you, Lily girl?" He touched my hair.

"What is more like me?" I asked genuinely curious. I still didn't remember all of who I was as an angel.

"I should have trusted and waited. I should have had faith in you that you wouldn't just leave me without really thinking it through."

"I love you, Andrew. I always loved you. Of course, I took it seriously." I sat up. Our time was coming to an end. I could feel the pain coming on and my head was killing me and there I was in the hospital room with my blue-eyed boy.

"Baby girl, I'm here waiting." I felt him take my hand. "I need you. Ruby needs you." He was crying and I wanted suddenly to be able to open my eyes and be with him.

Then, it was gone and I was with Andrew again. He was staring at me. He sat up next to me and kissed my shoulder.

"Why are you there?" he asked.

"I am there to save someone."

"You don't know, do you?" His face was tired.

"I can't just leave you here," I said.

"Then stay," he pleaded with me.

"No." I shook my head. "That wasn't what I meant. I have to see if anything can be done for so that . . ." I trailed off.

"So that you and I won't be a *fallen* angel. It's ok, say it." I felt fire coming from him.

"I need to go." I got up and put my clothes on. I walked slowly down the staircase. I was trapped between two worlds—one is a happy dream and the other is my worst nightmare. Andrew falling like this was my worst nightmare. I could feel Jason though and my heart ached as I got back to the loft and saw all of his imprints there. I kneeled down on the hardwood floor and wept.

CHAPTER SEVENTEEN

This time, Andrew had not followed and I knew why. He was ashamed to look at me right now or of me seeing him this way. I felt his pain and I felt my own. How did I live like this ever? I thought to myself.

"You never did." I jumped at Ian's voice.

"Really, Ian?" I looked up at him. "You scared me to death!" He went on as if I hadn't said anything.

"You never felt this much pain, Lily. You only ever felt his. You were never in pain. You are the happiest and most beautiful angel that there is."

"I'm not an angel right now," I said with a little bite. There was Lily, the human girl who didn't know what was happening. I still really didn't know.

"You are always an angel." Ian grinned. "You are going to try and save Andrew." It was a statement.

"What else can I do, Ian? I have to try." Now I felt tired.

"Ok, I will talk to Rose," he answered. Rose was a higher up. She sat in the throne room and watched over the humans. Right now, she would have to be my proxy.

"Spare me the speech on how he did this to himself. You love him too, Ian! He was your best friend!"

"I didn't say anything." He put his hands up. I cocked my head to one side and raised my eyebrow. "Ok, I will spare you and you are right. I do love him too."

"Yes." Ian was the most beautiful angel that I knew. He turned to leave but I had one more thing on my mind at that moment.

"Ian?" I called after him. He turned around and smiled at me.

"Yes, baby girl?"

"What am I doing here? In the world, I mean."

"You will have to ask Jason." He shook his head and walked out closing the door behind him. I was alone for the first time in a long time. I curled up on the couch and cried myself to sleep.

I woke up in the hospital in a panic. No! I was not ready for this! I opened my eyes and saw my boy.

"Hey," Jason said sweetly. He knew I was panicked. "Shhh . . . You are ok. I am here." He took my hand and I squeezed. It felt so good to feel him again. I thought I had lost him forever. Wait. This couldn't be it. I still had all of the knowledge that I had. I had heard Ian say that once. When I went back for good, I wouldn't remember the angels. So, I breathed and smiled at the cute boy that I had come to love so much, the only friend and family I had on the whole earth. I would be lying if I said that I didn't miss him so much and that I was so relieved to see him again and so happy that he was alive!

"Lily." Jason sat on the edge of my bed. "I am so sorry!" No, it wasn't time. I closed my eyes and let him hold me. I couldn't speak yet; I tried to but nothing came out. My throat was burning. Then, I realized that I had a tube down my throat. I started to grab at it. It was scary and uncomfortable. I could feel tears streaming down my cheeks.

"Baby girl," Jason was trying to calm me, "I'm here. There is a tube down your throat and I think they will take it out but I need you to breathe through your nose for me, ok?" He was holding my wrist lightly but firmly. He said all of that like it was completely normal for me to have a tube shoved down my throat. That was my

Jason. I wanted to smile at him but everything hurt. Then I let him take my hand and that warm calm came over me.

"I'm going to go get someone." He started to let go but I grabbed him. I was too afraid for him to leave. He didn't argue. He just came back and kept holding onto my hand. I kept breathing until I was back in the loft.

The sun was shining through my sheer curtains. *Why did I get sheer curtains?* I thought to myself, even though the thought was irrelevant anyway. I squinted and went straight to the coffee. My throat was still burning. It felt like the tube was still in there. I suppose technically, it still was.

Ok, Lily, just stop thinking for five minutes and have some coffee, I told myself. There was too much to worry about now that I knew and mostly understood what was happening. I was still so disappointed with Andrew, but at the same time, he had no idea who he was dealing with. He did not at all realize the danger that he was in. I was so angry with him for not trusting me. I took a sip of my coffee and decided that there was no more time to be mad at him. Soon, I would lose him forever maybe and I didn't want to leave things like this.

I sat down at the counter drinking my coffee and thinking. All I could think of was Andrew. I was so angry with the whole situation! Then, as if I needed more torture, there she was.

"Oh, Lily." Tempy was there in my living room. "Such a martyr."

"Tempy, what are you doing here?" I asked annoyed at her very presence.

"I am here for you." She flashed her red eyes at me. She could be so seductive when she wanted to be. That made me angry that she appeared to my love as a beautiful girl seducing him. I wanted to turn her into ashes. "You have no power here." She must have seen the look in my eye.

"Neither do you! Only your seductive, deceitful little butt." She was something else. Her face was burned and her eyes had turned red over time. Her red hair didn't really exist, I think so, but I didn't know what it really looked like. She was an ugly demon and one of the most powerful. That is why no one knew of her. The angels knew about the constant battle for power between the two kingdoms but they didn't know the royals. That was for their own safety.

"Somebody sounds jealous," she sang at me.

"Of course, I'm jealous! You made yourself look similar to me so that you could convince Andrew to make a deal with you. The thought of him being seduced by you at all makes me sick!" I spat out at her. I was never afraid to say what I felt or thought. The human Lily was bitter and mean anyway.

"I am after you," she repeated. "I know that you don't want to leave him. And you don't have to." She looked at me seriously now. "Come on, friend." Just as Ian and Andrew had been best friends once, so had Tempy and I. She was like a sister to me. Her burns were courtesy of me. When she fell with her father, she was given fire. Fire represented death and that was why Andrew always felt warm but he had never had fire. Now, he did have fire! It had to be a way of keeping him from me, except none of this was making any sense.

"He came running to me the second he knew that you were leaving. He begged me for help." She shrugged casually.

"There is no way that you are going to convince me to stay. Do you know why?" She just stood there waiting for me to go on. "Because I know what is really going to happen."

"So now, you are pleading for his life. You two are really two peas in a pod, aren't you?" She came toward me. "What if I told you that you and Andrew would just be stuck here in this place for all eternity?" She looked at me for a moment. "I told Andrew that you two would be able to return home but really, what if you could just stay here with your love never able to return home?"

"I would say that you are lying." There was always an agenda when it came to demons. She smiled at me.

"You think that I have one weakness," I said glaring at her.

"You do," she said confidently. Then, she was gone. I let out a sigh. I hated her to the bone! I sat and kept drinking my coffee in peace when a sight for sore eyes walked in.

"Doesn't anybody knock?" I exclaimed.

"No, we don't." It was Abel, my little brother.

"Hey!" I got up and hugged him on my tiptoes. Everyone was bigger than me except for Rose.

"What are you doing in the *veil*?" He asked with his hands on his hips.

"Andrew." I sat on the couch. "Why are you asking? You know exactly what is going on. You are with Rose in the throne room." If Abel was nothing else, he was always the fun one.

"That wouldn't be any fun now, would it?" He winked at me. "I'm glad that you know who I am."

"Well, little brother, I only just remembered you so don't get too cocky." I smiled at him. I had missed him. But I hadn't because I didn't know any of them were there for the last fifteen years and I would forget as soon as I left the veil for good.

"Andrew will be fine." He came and sat down next to me.

"Why did you come?" I asked. Surely, Rose or anyone else could have come to tell me.

"Because I wanted to see you." He grabbed my hand and squeezed. "Don't be so bitter, Lily. We are with you and soon, you will be home."

"You are worried about me?" I teased. He ran his hand through his hair and looked away. Superior being or not, Abel was still a boy.

"I know what you have been through. I have been watching." Compassion came into his eyes. "I will always be watching out for you."

"Thank you." I looked back with the same seriousness. He stood up and pulled me to my feet with him. He gave me a big hug. I started to cry into his shoulder.

"Hey, Andrew will be fine. He won't fall. But he will be stuck in the veil with a different job. A more painful job." He looked so serious for a boy who never is.

"I am glad. Thank you, guys," I managed between sobs.

"Then, why are you crying, love?" There was so much sincerity in his voice. I had forgotten what that even sounded like.

"I am going to lose him forever all because he wasn't patient enough to listen to my entire explanation." Then, I laughed through my tears a little. "An explanation I still don't know the entirety of." Abel held me by the shoulders at arm's length.

"It's a good one." He smiled. Then, more tears came.

"This was all a test of our faith and he failed. He chose me!" I couldn't stop crying and I threw myself back into my beloved little brother's arms. Most girls would want that. Any human girl would be grateful to be chosen above all else. But we were not human.

"You are literally his other half, Lily. What did you expect? Not all of us can be as strong as you are sometimes."

"I don't feel very strong right now." I pouted at him.

"But you are, and I love you."

He kissed my forehead and left. It was good to see that boy.

CHAPTER EIGHTEEN

I took a walk to the bridge. I had no idea what I was hoping to find there but I had to get out. I wanted Andrew but I didn't know if he would come. He was so embarrassed to see me. I wished he wouldn't feel that way.

I stood on the bridge listening to the water hit the rocks just like the day Andrew had saved me from jumping. Now I knew what he had meant when he said, "Not this way." I stood there and looked out over the beautiful land when I felt his presence next to me.

"I was waiting for you," I said without looking at him.

"I know." We took each other's hands still kept on the railing.

"This bridge." I couldn't get any farther without wanting to cry. I wanted to cry for Andrew and for Jason and even little Ruby. I still didn't know how she fit into all of this. This entire thing was a big puzzle.

"Stop it," Andrew nudged.

"Stop what?" I turned to look at him. He was so amazing to look at.

"Taking on the weight of the universe." He laughed a little.

"The weight of the world." I corrected. But I knew what he was trying to say and he was right. "I am still missing a piece."

"I know but you will find the missing piece." I went back to looking at all of the beautiful pine trees. This was my veil. This was all created for me and the fortress was there for Andrew but it was there for me too.

"No, I will not." We both knew it did not work that way. We were created together and now the darkness had torn us apart.

"I know."

"I am so sad." I slid over closer to him. "Andrew, they wanted me. They were never going to let us go home or stay here. The whole point of you making that deal was to get me to come to the fire of the dark kingdom. That was your fate too."

"I know that too," he said with the coldness I knew so well. He had never been cold before like this. He was tired and he saw a lot of horrible things, so he looked tired a lot but never cold. He always had a light in his eyes with me. Now, that light was gone. It made me sad.

I doubled over in pain suddenly. My eyes started to water and I was screaming. What was happening? Andrew was there beside me trying to hold me but I kept pushing him away. I heard him calling for Ian and I was scared. Good. I remember thinking, Ian would help. The pain did not subside and I was still on the bridge not hearing voices or seeing things. What was happening to me? I felt Ian lifting me up as I continued to scream. I could feel Andrew's worries. I could feel everything. I could feel Jason and Ruby. Wait! Ruby, something was wrong with Ruby.

Eventually, the pain subsided and I was still resting outside on the bridge with Ian and Andrew. Ian looked fine and Andrew looked terrified.

"Ian," I started, "I have to get back." I could not help but see the pain in Andrew's eyes.

"I know you do, baby girl."

"It's Ruby, isn't it?" I asked

"Yes, it is." He only looked at me.

"I need to see Jason." The words just came out. I hadn't even thought about Andrew or anyone else being there. I just had an urgency to get back to my friend. But I was still afraid.

"Don't be afraid, baby girl. You go do what you need to do. What you set out to do all along." He half-smiled. I looked at Andrew.

"Go, Lily girl," Andrew said. "Please don't be afraid. I can still feel you from here." I wasn't sure if that was a good thing or a bad thing.

"Wait, I need some time with Andrew first." I took Andrew by the hand and we walked back to the courtyard where I first saw him, well sort of. We walked and lingered.

"What is going to happen to me?" He turned to look at me directly.

"My father will let you stay here in our veil." *Our veil*—somehow, those words made it sound more special. "They have a new job for you but I don't know what it is." I looked down at our hands holding onto each other.

"What will happen with us?" he asked pulling me into his chest.

"I don't know, my love," I whispered and fought the sadness, the deepest and darkest sadness that was beginning to build up in me. I closed my eyes and took in the moment—every smell, every sound, and every feeling. I knew it didn't matter because soon, it would all be gone from my memory. "Come on." I pulled away and we walked back to the loft where Ian was waiting for us.

When we got there, the door was open. I walked in and saw Ian immediately. He smiled at me lovingly and then something interesting occurred. He nodded his head to Andrew. I could feel Andrew tense up immediately. Only I knew that it was because Andrew felt so ashamed of himself. I was never one to speak for Andrew and I was not about to start now.

"I am sorry, Ian." Well, that was a first. Even Ian looked shocked.

"There is nothing to be sorry for." Ian smiled without skipping a beat. Then, I finally asked the question that had secretly been bothering me. I felt as though I was dreaming all of this time even though I knew it was real, but there were two realities that I was living through right now. Somehow, Andrew had made that possible. The veil is a place where you don't know reality. It is a safe place between life and death and here, I was living a nightmare because beloved Andrew had screwed up. I was not angry really; just hurt and confused. So, I asked, "Where is Lily?" It was a serious question. Was I still on the bridge or was I in the hospital like I saw in my visions? No. Those were definitely not visions I was there.

"You have to ask Jason," Ian answered once again.

"Why do you keep saying that?" I was only slightly irritated. "Why can't you just tell me, Ian?" We all stood there looking at each other. Then Ian sighed.

"I can't tell you, Lily, because you haven't made a decision yet."

"Yes, I have!" I had, why was he saying that?

"No, Lily, the moment you make the decision to leave here, you will be gone." I knew what he was saying was true. I knew that I was delaying leaving my Andrew behind. It never occurred to me at the time that I would not remember any of this for a while anyway because I have been living in all sorts of realms and decades and centuries. I knew that eventually, I would remember losing Andrew.

We all stood in a circle in front of my open doorway. We were all together again under the worst circumstances ever. Andrew looked at each of us and then walked out the door. I wanted to let him go. I didn't want the pain of another goodbye. I could not do it. I could not just leave it like this, so I followed him.

I sat with Andrew on the bench. His heat was radiating but I was curled up next to him like I usually did. This entire thing had been one big nightmare! Maybe that is all it will ever be to me.

"I screwed up." Andrew stared straight ahead. His eyes were getting darker by the second and he was growing hotter by second.

"You did," I said in an emotionless way. I had to be. Otherwise, I would completely fall apart.

"You chose him." He looked at me with great sadness.

"I never chose him. Don't you know by now, Andrew? I love you!"

"Then, why do you never choose me?" My heart sank and I took his fiery hand but my hand was cold again.

"I always choose to do the right thing." I could not believe that my angel was going to live in this eternity of sadness and hell. He had already been a sad angel and now, he was stuck here. No, I could not blame myself for this. He did this.

"Lily, I am so sorry that I failed you." For the first time, I saw tears spilling over onto his cheeks.

"They were after me. They knew that you were the way to do it." I threw my arms around his neck. "The darkness will never win. I love you always," I whispered in his ear. We sat there holding onto each other for what would feel like never enough time.

"Hey," Ian came up to us. He sounded sad too. Maybe he was. We all were.

"Time?" I asked without looking up.

"Yes," he answered sadly.

"I took care of everything. Tell Rose, ok?" I was looking at Andrew.

"That is your humanity coming out," Andrew said coldly. "There is nothing to worry about, Lily girl."

"You are really going to let me leave like this?" Andrew was never cold with me. I hated this more than he would ever know. He stood up and lifted me into his arms.

"Always be cold for me," he whispered into my hair. "My Lily girl."

"Always."

CHAPTER NINETEEN

I woke up in the hospital bed. This time, I was nothing more than a bitter girl. I struggled with the tube in my throat and Jason called for the nurse.

"Oh, baby!" He rushed to my side and kissed my forehead. "Just breathe, baby girl." He soothed and everything seemed to calm down. They took the tube out of my throat. I guess that I hadn't been breathing on my own. My voice was scratchy and I really couldn't talk much but I knew what was happening. Ruby was sick and she was mine. She was my little sister and that was why the foster parents had found me.

"Ruby," I whispered. I tried to move.

"No, baby girl." Jason sat on the bed next to me with his hands on my arms gently. "You woke up!" His relief was confusing to me. What had happened? Where was I? The monitor next to me started beeping like crazy.

"Hey." Jason looked into my eyes and I saw calm there once again. "You are ok. You have been in a coma and I thought you were gone!"

"Ruby?" Why was I thinking about Ruby? My chest started to hurt and this time, no one could stop it or help me.

"She is here." He was still sounding surprised that I was asking about her. "Lily, she is dying."

"What?" I whispered. My voice was hoarse and my throat burned.

"Dawn came to find us and, on the way, Ruby had a bad spell. Both of her kidneys are failing." Tears were in his eyes. My little sister was dying? That was why they wanted to find me. Did they think I could help somehow?

When I finally focused, I looked around the room I was in. There was glass everywhere and I could see all the nurses and doctors buzzing around right outside. A little blonde nurse came in and smiled at me.

"You are awake." She sounded happy. How could anyone possibly sound happy while I was hooked up to machines and my whole body was hurting?

"She is." Jason smiled at me. Those beautiful eyes were the ones I could not be angry at. Why was I here? I had no memory after leaving the foster home that night. I only knew that I had found my biological family and that beautiful little girl was sick the way I had been sick my entire life. I had a funny feeling like I had just woken up from a dream that I could not remember.

"Ruby," I whispered.

"Shh . . . Baby girl. You can see her when you gain some strength." I looked past him and saw Dawn standing outside my room. We locked eyes and she came in.

"Jason," she started sweetly, "can I have a minute alone with Lily?" Jason looked at me and I closed my eyes.

"I will be right outside," he said squeezing my hand. Dawn, the foster mother, the woman who gave birth to me and then brought me into her home selfishly, only to let me be abused. I felt the anger of the last fifteen years rising up inside me.

"Lily, I messed up." She sounded small and broken. I did not look at her. I couldn't. I had hated this woman since the day I was born and now, I hated her more. "I am so sorry." I would not open my eyes. I could hear her voice cracking. "You grew up to be such a beautiful girl." There was no apology for what she had done or put me through. I could not forgive her.

She sat there with me in silence for a long time while I kept my eyes closed. The tears were escaping from under my eyelids and I knew that I was listening. She let out a long sigh and finally, I heard her stand up.

"I am sorry." I heard her choking back tears. What was she sorry for? Was it for abandoning me to live a terrible harmful life? Or for finding and bringing me into a home to be completely torn apart physically, mentally, and emotionally? Or could it possibly be for being so selfish to bring me into that situation only to help the daughter that she really loved? None of it mattered to me. I did not want her apologies. I heard her talking to Jason about Ruby as she left the room.

"She won't even look at me," I heard her say to Jason, but Jason was silent. He was my Jason and he was on my side no matter what.

"Do you blame her, Dawn?" was all he said and then he was back at my side. I opened my eyes. We looked at each other and he smiled. "You came back to me." I smiled back a little. Then, the pain came and I moaned.

"Here." He showed me a button to press and I felt calm and warm as the pain faded. I couldn't keep my eyes open and I let myself drift to sleep.

CHAPTER TWENTY

When I woke again, I was still in the hospital room. I could not tell how long I had been asleep. The room was dark save for the little lights that were on in the hospital. I looked to my right and Jason was asleep in a chair next to me. I reached out and touched his hand. His hand was warm or I was cold but he opened his eyes and sat up.

"Lily." He leaned onto my bed. I felt strangely weak like I was about to pass out.

"Ruby," I said in a little above a whisper.

"You need to rest." I shook my head. "Do you want to see her?" For a moment, I couldn't answer. I was staring at the bottom of my bed where Ian was standing, my majestic guardian angel. He smiled at me and I smiled back. When I looked back at Jason, he looked afraid. He did not move from my side.

"Ruby." I tried to be more persistent in my weakened state. Something was happening and I did not want Jason to be here.

"Ok, I'll go get her." I tried to reach for him. He seemed to understand and came down close to me.

"I love you," I whispered in his ear.

"I love you too, baby girl." His eyes started to fill with tears. He looked like he was afraid and wanted to leave my side suddenly.

"Go." I tried to smile. "Come on. Stop being a pain." He reluctantly left me to go get Ruby. When I looked again, Ian was gone. The heart monitor slowed and I saw his face once more. It was beautiful and I thought I was dreaming. There is a thin veil between life and death. Now, for the first time, I knew I was about to cross the veil to home. I took his hand.

"Will this help her?" I asked.

"Yes." His eyes were cold and instead of walking with him, I passed through him and I felt all of his pain.

www.ingramcontent.com/pod-product-compliance
Lightning Source LLC
Chambersburg PA
CBHW020322030826
48979CB00022B/703

* 9 7 8 1 9 5 5 1 5 6 9 3 6 *